A Burial Place

by Owen Panettieri

FOR PRODUCTION INQUIRIES

UNITED STATES AND CANADA
info@concordtheatricals.com
1-866-979-0447

UNITED KINGDOM AND EUROPE
licensing@concordtheatricals.co.uk
020-7054-7298

Each title is subject to availability from Concord Theatricals Corp., depending upon country of performance. Please be aware that *A BURIAL PLACE* may not be licensed by Concord Theatricals Corp. in your territory. Professional and amateur producers should contact the nearest Concord Theatricals Corp. office or licensing partner to verify availability.

This work is published by Samuel French, an imprint of Concord Theatricals Corp.

No one shall make any changes in this title(s) for the purpose of production. No part of this book may be reproduced, stored in a retrieval system, scanned, uploaded, or transmitted in any form, by any means, now known or yet to be invented, including mechanical, electronic, digital, photocopying, recording, videotaping, or otherwise, without the prior written permission of the publisher. No one shall share this title(s), or any part of this title(s), through any social media or file hosting websites.

For all inquiries regarding motion picture, television, online/digital and other media rights, please contact Concord Theatricals Corp.

MUSIC AND THIRD-PARTY MATERIALS USE NOTE

Licensees are solely responsible for obtaining formal written permission from copyright owners to use copyrighted music and/or other copyrighted third-party materials (e.g. artworks, logos) in the performance of this play and are strongly cautioned to do so. If no such permission is obtained by the licensee, then the licensee must use only original music and materials that the licensee owns and controls. Licensees are solely responsible and liable for clearances of all third-party copyrighted materials, including without limitation music, and shall indemnify the copyright owners of the play(s) and their licensing agent, Concord Theatricals Corp., against any costs, expenses, losses and liabilities arising from the use of such copyrighted third-party materials by licensees. For music, please contact the appropriate music licensing authority in your territory for the rights to any incidental music.

IMPORTANT BILLING AND CREDIT REQUIREMENTS

If you have obtained performance rights to this title, please refer to your licensing agreement for important billing and credit requirements.

A BURIAL PLACE was first produced by New Light Theater Project in association with 5000 Broadway Productions, premiering at the Dorothy Strelsin Theatre, New York City, on November 3, 2016. The producers were Luis A. Miranda Jr. and Sarah Norris. The production was directed by Joey Brenneman, with scenic design by Ashleigh Poteat, sound design by Andy Evan Cohen, lighting design by Ali Hall, and prop design by Charlotte Harrison. Technical direction was provided by Jen Medina-Gray and press representation was provided by Charlie Guadano. The production stage manager was Allyson Namishia and the assistant stage manager was Connor Scully. The cast was as follows:

EMMETT... Evan Maltby

COLBY...Max King

MARCUS... Deshawn Wyatte

CHARACTERS

EMMETT – Sensitive, fantasy-loving college kid, 19, Male

COLBY – Emmett's jaded high school ex-boyfriend, 19, Male

MARCUS – Childhood best friend of Emmett and Colby. A bright spirit. Black, 19, Male

NOTE: Emmett and Colby can be portrayed by non-Black actors of any race/ethnicity.

SETTING

Childhood clubhouse on Emmett's family's property.

TIME

June 2015, in the evening.

NOTE

A / indicates that the next line of dialogue should begin while the current line continues to its completion.

PLAYWRIGHT'S NOTE

In writing *A Burial Place*, I was taken by the idea of how young people might process loss even when they lack the definitive answers needed to help them make sense of things. When the fate of someone we love remains unresolved, it feels impossible to move on, but time still moves us forward.

When the world won't provide you with closure, is it possible to create closure for yourself? Can magic exist in a world of harsh reality? Are the stories we tell ourselves to help us get through the day actually hurting us? How do we make peace with our mistakes? Emmett, Colby, and Marcus must find answers to these questions for themselves, but hopefully they can support each other on their respective journeys. To that end, the play is not about uncovering what happened to Marcus in the past. It's about finding a way forward. In terms of what is going on with Marcus, it's my hope that future directors and casts will examine the text and make the choices that feel right for them.

The play takes place in 2015. If you are not familiar with the pop culture references the characters talk about, look them up! These characters, movies, games, and shows mean a lot to them and provide additional insights into who they are and what matters to them.

I want to say thank you to the tremendous cast and crew of the original production of *A Burial Place*. Thank you to Sarah Norris at New Light Theater Project and Luis A. Miranda Jr. at 5000 Broadway Productions for their keen judgement and support while producing the initial run of the show. Thank you to Kim Sharp and Bara Swain for their early support of my work and to Bryson Bruce for his perspective on the play in its early development. I am forever in debt to Joey Brenneman for her amazing original direction. And finally, a big thank you to Josh Blye for being my incredible sounding board, my champion, and my partner in experiencing life's wonders. They say we are birds of a feather.

For Phil and Steph, and for the Circle of Friends

Scene One

(The interior of a suburban detached garage. In former lives it was a small barn, a shed, a children's clubhouse and a converted home office. It is currently used for storage. This structure is set back from the main house on the property. The year is 2015, early summer. **EMMETT**, *19, organizes the clutter in the room, setting up for a sleepover. He has a good heart and a practiced smile. His outfit appears casual, but he's spent a lot of time considering his clothes, his underwear, his hair, and especially how he smells in anticipation of his two guests. Two sleeping bags, snacks and games are stacked on a folding table. He hangs a few wire dry-cleaning hangers on a nail in the wall and checks his phone for the time. He considers a large plastic container in the room and moves a large box in front of it. He picks up an assortment of sports balls that's more than he can easily handle. While* **EMMETT***'s back is to the door,* **COLBY**, *also 19, enters the garage.* **COLBY** *looks like he doesn't care how he looks, content to get by on his undeniably charming smile. The sound of the door startles* **EMMETT**, *who drops what he's holding, balls bouncing away from him. He tries to recover them. He's flailing and looks ridiculous.)*

EMMETT. Oh, hey!

COLBY. You okay there?

EMMETT. Yeah, I'm fine!

COLBY. I didn't mean to scare you.

EMMETT. You didn't!

COLBY. No?

EMMETT. No! It's just – you're early.

> (**COLBY** *checks his phone.* **EMMETT** *goes back to organizing things, avoiding eye contact.*)

COLBY. It's seven.

EMMETT. No, it's a quarter to seven.

COLBY. Okay...well, that's basically seven.

EMMETT. I figured I had at least a half hour before you'd show up.

COLBY. Oh yeah?

EMMETT. Yeah. When are you ever on time for anything? Forget about early.

COLBY. Emmett, can you stop for a minute?

EMMETT. What?

> (**EMMETT** *looks at* **COLBY**, *who extends his arms for a hug.*)

COLBY. Hi.

EMMETT. Hi, Colby.

> (*They hug. It's a little longer than* **EMMETT** *would like and he pulls away first.*)

COLBY. Hey, you smell good!

EMMETT. I do?

COLBY. Yeah, what do you got on?

EMMETT. Uh, deodorant?

COLBY. Okay. I thought maybe it was, like, fancy.

EMMETT. Yeah, because all this is very fancy.

> (**EMMETT** *turns away to stack boxes.* **COLBY** *takes the opportunity to check out* **EMMETT**'s *ass. He's in better shape than* **COLBY** *anticipated.*)

COLBY. Obviously. So how was the end of semester for you?

EMMETT. It was fine. You?

COLBY. Fine. How'd that play go?

EMMETT. Oh, it was fine. No big deal.

COLBY. I'm sorry I missed your stage debut.

EMMETT. No. I didn't have a big part.

COLBY. Are you still writing?

EMMETT. Yeah. Of course.

COLBY. I just didn't know if maybe you were leaning more toward acting now.

EMMETT. No, this was just something I did. It counted as class credit, so...

COLBY. Good. I like your writing.

EMMETT. Well, don't worry. I'm doing it.

> (**EMMETT** *goes back to cleaning. The sexual energy between them intensifies.*)

COLBY. Good. When'd you get back?

EMMETT. Last week.

COLBY. Lucky. You guys get out so early.

EMMETT. It's like three days difference from you.

COLBY. I guess. Your hair looks good like that.

EMMETT. Oh.

(He fixes it self-consciously.)

COLBY. What? It does. Did you just get it cut?

EMMETT. No. Why?

COLBY. I haven't seen any pictures of it like that online, is all.

EMMETT. You Facebook stalking me, now?

COLBY. Instagram, mostly.

EMMETT. Ha.

COLBY. Don't be a dick, Emmett. Okay?

EMMETT. I'm not being –

COLBY. Just breathe.

EMMETT. I am breathing.

COLBY. You're not breathing.

EMMETT. Then how am I talking?

COLBY. One of life's many mysteries.

(A pause.)

We're good, right?

EMMETT. Yeah! I'm good! Totally. We're totally good.

(He smiles and goes back to cleaning. They are not good.)

COLBY. I can't believe it's been six months. That's gotta be a record, huh?

EMMETT. I'd say so. Are you hanging around for the summer, or are you going up to camp again?

COLBY. Camp in a couple weeks. Senior staff now.

EMMETT. That's scary.

COLBY. Tell me about it. What are you doing? You working at Harlan's again?

EMMETT. I don't know. I might pick up shifts there for a couple weeks. We're supposed to go on a trip to Spain in late July – family trip –

COLBY. Oh? That's awesome.

EMMETT. Yeah! But now we don't know, with the news and all. You know...

COLBY. Why should that stop you guys from going away?

EMMETT. In case there's a hearing, or we need to testify... I don't know. It's still not settled when we're leaving.

COLBY. Well, I'm sure you don't have to cancel your plans –

EMMETT. We're just not sure yet, is all.

COLBY. So *that's* what's got you freaking out. The news.

EMMETT. No. I just want things to be settled for Marcus when he shows up.

(**COLBY** *looks over the supplies.*)

COLBY. You got a lot of stuff here, Emm. You didn't have to do that.

EMMETT. What do you mean? It's the standard fare.

COLBY. Two sleeping bags?

EMMETT. This one's mine and this is for Marcus. Did you leave your stuff in the car?

COLBY. Emmett...

EMMETT. What?

COLBY. C'mon, man...

EMMETT. You didn't bring anything?

COLBY. I did not.

EMMETT. You want me to go get blankets from the house?

COLBY. No, I figured –

EMMETT. You figured what?

COLBY. We're not really doing this tonight, are we?

EMMETT. ...What?

COLBY. Emmett. We're not doing this.

EMMETT. Are you serious? How can – *this* is why you're here early? You're not staying at all?

COLBY. I'm here because I want us to talk. Face to face –

EMMETT. Oh, fucking great.

COLBY. Will you not roll your eyes at me? I'm serious. Let's talk about this.

EMMETT. Fine. Go ahead, Colby. I'm listening.

COLBY. Look. I know why you're doing this.

EMMETT. Yeah, I'd hope so.

COLBY. We're getting a little old for this, don't you think? Maybe it's time we let go of the group sleepover.

EMMETT. You're a shit. You know that?

COLBY. I'm not! I'm not trying to be.

EMMETT. What are we supposed to tell Marcus when he shows up?

COLBY. You think he's gonna show?

EMMETT. Yes, Colby. Of course he will. This isn't just some random get together. You're really gonna stand there and act like –

COLBY. I know what day it is. I just meant...with *recent developments* and all...

EMMETT. Even more reason why we should be here for him tonight! We're his best friends. He needs us to be supportive.

> (**EMMETT** *starts shoving things around the room more aggressively.*)

COLBY. Emm, come on.

EMMETT. I cannot believe you.

> (**COLBY** *moves to reach out to him.*)

Please don't attempt to touch me right now.

> (**COLBY** *retreats. They stand in silence for a moment.*)

COLBY. What's your dad using this place for now, anyway?

EMMETT. Mostly storage, right now.

COLBY. What about all his photography stuff? He still does that, right?

EMMETT. Yeah, he moved it into the house for a while. He had to repair part of the roof out here last fall after the hurricane.

COLBY. Does it leak?

EMMETT. No, it's fine now. He just hasn't moved back in yet.

COLBY. Alright.

EMMETT. It's not going to rain. Besides I thought you weren't staying.

COLBY. *(He smiles at **EMMETT**.)* Can I have some snacks?

EMMETT. You're unbelievable.

COLBY. I didn't have dinner!

EMMETT. Oh, were you planning on getting something after your little drive by appearance? You have a hot date?

COLBY. God, Emmett. I didn't eat because I was nervous. Okay? I was nervous about coming here. I always am.

EMMETT. Take what you want from the table.

> (**COLBY** *goes over and takes a closer look at the goodies.*)

COLBY. Ugh, you always do this. You bring out the ingredients for s'mores but there's no fire in here for us to make s'mores. Unless...

> (*He notices a metal garbage can in the corner, moves toward it.* **EMMETT** *cuts off his path.*)

EMMETT. My dad is not gonna let us start a fire in here.

COLBY. Then why bring this stuff?

EMMETT. Because I like the ingredients! Where are your brownies?

> (**COLBY** *shrugs and backs off, embarrassed.*)

You didn't even bring those? That's really great.

COLBY. I asked my mom to make them, but she was busy... What are your folks doing tonight?

EMMETT. Nothing. They're inside.

COLBY. They don't think it's weird that I'm coming over here?

EMMETT. I didn't really talk to them about it. They know it's tradition.

COLBY. Should I go in and say hi?

EMMETT. Do you want to?

COLBY. I don't know. I just don't want to be rude. I should've said hi, right?

EMMETT. They won't care.

COLBY. I just thought maybe they... I dunno, ask about me?

EMMETT. They don't. They give me space. Look, we don't have to rehash everything okay? Can we put that aside for this evening and just be here for Marcus?

COLBY. Yeah, we can...but –

EMMETT. But you don't think he's gonna show. You thought that last year too.

COLBY. His parents were back on the news yesterday. You see that?

EMMETT. I saw it. His mom came over the day before I got home to give my folks a heads-up.

COLBY. So what do you think?

EMMETT. What they have is inconclusive. There's no evidence linking him –

COLBY. They think the timeline checks out.

EMMETT. Well, they want to believe it does.

COLBY. No, not just his mom. I mean the *cops* think the timeline fits.

EMMETT. It's not that cut and dry. And suddenly you're a fan of the cops?

COLBY. I'm just saying, you think they're all wrong?

EMMETT. I think it's very early. They've been through a lot and I just don't want them to be let down again for a false lead.

COLBY. Okay, so what are we gonna do about it tonight, assuming he shows?

EMMETT. We'll ask him what he thinks.

COLBY. And if he doesn't want to talk about it, like Marcus never wants to talk about it?

EMMETT. Then we talk about normal shit. Whatever he wants. That's the deal. Right?

COLBY. Right... Is the TV still hooked up out here?

EMMETT. No, it broke.

COLBY. Ugh, you're kidding!

EMMETT. That thing was older than we are.

COLBY. We had it hooked up to the GameCube. It wasn't that old.

EMMETT. Well, it broke. My dad junked it.

COLBY. Do you still have the GameCube?

EMMETT. Yeah, it's in one of those boxes.

COLBY. The games too?

(**COLBY** *goes to look, alarming* **EMMETT**.)

EMMETT. Yeah. No, come on, Colby. I just cleared that space out. You're gonna make a mess. / We can't play it without the TV anyway.

COLBY. I'm not gonna make a mess. *Babe*, I just wanted to look at the old games!

EMMETT. There are games in that box, okay? And no, "Babe."

COLBY. Would've been fun to play *Mario Kart* tonight to pass the time.

EMMETT. Because you're so good at *Mario Kart*?

COLBY. I am! That and *Smash Bros*. That's where I dominated.

EMMETT. Yeah, okay. Can you push those boxes up against the wall for me?

(**COLBY** *does so. He starts humming a theme song.**)

---

* A license to produce *A Burial Place* does not include a performance license for any third-party or copyrighted music. Licensees should create an original composition or use music in the public domain. For further information, please see the Music and Third-Party Materials Use Note on page iii.

What's that?

COLBY. It's the theme to *Smash Bros.*

EMMETT. That's not how it goes. It's:

(**EMMETT** *hums a different tune.**)

COLBY. I was humming the main theme, not the battle theme.

EMMETT. I'm humming the main theme!

(*He hums it again.* **COLBY** *hums his version over* **EMMETT**'s *version. They are beginning to annoy the fuck out of each other the way only loved ones can do.* **COLBY** *picks up a soft toy from one of the boxes and throws it at* **EMMETT**.)

COLBY. Ahh, enough! Stick to plays instead of musicals at school. You can't hold a simple melody.

(**EMMETT** *throws him back the toy.*)

EMMETT. I was singing it exactly right. Put this back in the box, please?

COLBY. Your dad is wasting this space. He should give it back to you.

EMMETT. What do I need it for?

COLBY. I don't know. It just looked awesome as our clubhouse and now it has no definition.

EMMETT. It looks cool when his photography is hanging up in here.

COLBY. Our setup was better. Were you able to get beer?

EMMETT. Yeah, it's in those shopping bags under there.

COLBY. Nice!

(*He gets one. Opens it. Takes a sip.*)

COLBY. So…do we have access to the Dungeon?

EMMETT. The *crawl space* remains inaccessible.

COLBY. *Crawl space?* Very proper of you, Emm.

EMMETT. You know my mom's always hated us calling it the Dungeon.

COLBY. Hey, the Dungeon was awesome.

EMMETT. Okay.

COLBY. The time capsule's still under there.

EMMETT. I *know*. And that's where it's gonna stay.

COLBY. Such bullshit. Come on. Let's go get it.

> (**COLBY** *picks up a shovel leaning against the wall.*)

EMMETT. We can't get down there! My dad put mesh down there to keep the raccoons out.

> (**COLBY** *retreats, considering the shovel. He suddenly looks sad. He drinks his beer.*)

What's wrong?

COLBY. Nothing. What's your plan for entertainment if there's no TV?

EMMETT. I've got games.

COLBY. What do you have?

EMMETT. There's Life, obviously.

COLBY. Life takes like three hours to play.

EMMETT. One of its big selling points when there's no TV. You know Marcus is gonna make us play it.

COLBY. What else? Didn't you get, Settlers of Catan for Christmas?

EMMETT. Yeah, because *that's* a quick game.

COLBY. So what? Let's play that instead!

EMMETT. I'm not sure Marcus will like that one.

COLBY. He will. He picks things up quick.

(*He checks his phone.*)

EMMETT. I don't know if we can really play it with three players. Who are you texting?

COLBY. God, nobody! Like I'd get any reception out here. I was just checking the time. He's late.

EMMETT. No, he seems late to you because you're never here early.

(**EMMETT** *continues to organize games on the table.*)

COLBY. Did you bring out your Pokémon cards?

EMMETT. Why? You hate Pokémon.

COLBY. Well, watching you two play is the easiest way to fall asleep out here.

EMMETT. So now you're staying over?

COLBY. If he shows and he's staying, I'll stay.

EMMETT. And you're not gonna launch right into him, right? You'll go with the flow?

COLBY. Fine. As long as I'm not forced to play Pokémon.

EMMETT. Well, I left the cards up in my room anyway.

COLBY. What's that box?

EMMETT. Chess and checkers set.

COLBY. Ooh, strip checkers!

EMMETT. We are not playing strip checkers.

COLBY. My greatest invention! Not even once for old time's sake? While we wait?

EMMETT. Go sit your ass over on that side of the room, please, and calm yourself down.

COLBY. You're saying no 'cause you know I'd win.

EMMETT. There's no skill involved in Strip Checkers!

COLBY. No skill? That's not a very generous recollection, Emmett.

EMMETT. Stop it, Colby.

COLBY. You don't want to "King me"?

EMMETT. I mean it. You are being very inappropriate right now.

COLBY. I'm just kidding around. / We can't kid?

EMMETT. Well, I really don't appreciate kidding like that. Don't smile at me like that.

> (**COLBY** *leans in mischievously.* **EMMETT** *crosses his arms in front of his chest.*)

Don't try to pinch me, Colby!

COLBY. I'm not!

EMMETT. Back up. Back up back up back up!

> (*The side door swings open.* **MARCUS**, *19, enters wearing a Penn State T-shirt and jeans and a light jacket.*[*] *He has a sleeping bag slung over his shoulder. He's got a great smile and a peaceful vibe.* **EMMETT** *and* **COLBY** *stop, stare at him.*)

MARCUS. Somebody call for backup?

COLBY. Marcus! Hey...

---

[*] A license to produce *A Burial Place* does not include a license to publicly display any branded logos or trademarked images. Licensees must acquire rights for any logos and/or images or create their own.

EMMETT. Marcus!

(**EMMETT** *rushes over to* **MARCUS** *and they share a big hug.*)

MARCUS. S'up, Nerd Academy?

(*They separate and* **COLBY** *gives* **MARCUS** *a handshake one-arm-bro-hug.*)

S'up, State School? You look way too surprised to see me.

COLBY. Well, you're late, so I thought maybe you weren't showing.

MARCUS. It's like five minutes past. Calm yourself. I'm on time.

EMMETT. Told you.

MARCUS. Why are you torturing this kid?

COLBY. I'm not!

(**MARCUS** *pinches* **COLBY**'s *nipple and twists.*)

Ow!

MARCUS. Keep your hands to yourself.

COLBY. Alright! I wasn't doing anything.

MARCUS. Everything good?

EMMETT. Yeah. You brought your own bag!

MARCUS. Oh, yeah! Pretty sweet, huh?

COLBY. Where'd you get it?

MARCUS. There's this amazing new place called, "The store." They've got all this amazing stuff there. You should check it out.

COLBY. Oh, yeah? Sounds awesome.

EMMETT. You just never bring your own stuff.

MARCUS. Well, I don't need to mooch this year. My mom got it for me. Study abroad in the fall. Backpacking beforehand. Wanted me to travel in style. Figured I'd break it in tonight though.

COLBY. How's your mom doing?

MARCUS. A nag as always, but she's fine. And Murray is Murray. They're doing good. How's your sister doing in DC?

EMMETT. Jamie's good! She's got a job at NBC News now.

COLBY. Get out! That's awesome. What's she doing with them?

EMMETT. She's in research. Fact checking type stuff. She likes it a lot.

MARCUS. Are your folks home? I knocked to say hi to them before I came back, but nobody answered.

EMMETT. They're probably just upstairs with the TV on.

COLBY. So Marcus, how was school? Dean's List again this year?

MARCUS. Obviously. Killed it again. Spring was really good. I've got some amazing stories for you.

> (**MARCUS** *looks at* **EMMETT** *as if his eyes are refocusing on him.*)

> (*It's quick, but the* **BOYS** *notice it.*)

Hey! How was your big stage debut?

EMMETT. Oh, it was fine.

MARCUS. I totally would've been there if it weren't for finals. I wanted to take the bus up so bad. I'm sure you killed it.

(*To* **COLBY**.) Did you read the review? They raved about him.

COLBY. There was a review? What review?

EMMETT. School paper. It wasn't anything –

COLBY. You told me it was just a little part.

MARCUS. Dude, he was Konstantin in *The Seagull*.

COLBY. Okay, I don't know what that means. Is that the lead?

MARCUS. It's a big part.

EMMETT. He's blowing it out of proportion.

COLBY. Why wouldn't you just tell me that?

EMMETT. Because you didn't need to be there, so I didn't make a big deal about it.

MARCUS. They're putting up one of his own plays in the fall too.

COLBY. A play you wrote?

EMMETT. It's just a student production. A buddy of mine –

COLBY. So?

EMMETT. So Marcus made it sound like it was a department show or something, and it's not.

MARCUS. It's still really cool, man. That's what you went there to do and you're doing it.

COLBY. Is it one I've read?

EMMETT. No, it's new.

COLBY. What's it about?

EMMETT. It's hard to describe. It's kinda... It's magical realism.

COLBY. What's that? Like the Mizaki movies you like?

MARCUS. Miyazaki.

COLBY. *Thanks.* So is that it?

EMMETT. Kinda. Not really.

COLBY. Will you send it to me?

EMMETT. We'll see. I have to do another rewrite on it over the summer.

COLBY. I don't understand why I have to find this stuff out through *Marcus*.

MARCUS. Hey, did they record *Seagull*? Do you have a copy?

EMMETT. Yeah…

MARCUS. Then let's watch it!

EMMETT. Ha! No.

MARCUS. Why not?

EMMETT. There's no TV out here anymore.

MARCUS. We don't have the TV?

COLBY. Then let's go inside and watch it.

(**EMMETT** *shoots* **COLBY** *a warning look.*)

EMMETT. I don't think that's a good idea.

COLBY. Why not? If your folks are upstairs we won't be bothering them.

EMMETT. I don't want to watch it, Colby. I don't like watching myself. *Can we drop it?*

MARCUS. Sorry, Emm… I like your haircut!

EMMETT. Thanks.

(**COLBY** *gives* **MARCUS**' *look more consideration.*)

COLBY. What's happening with yours? It's cute. You're growing it out?

MARCUS. Nah. I was seeing this girl and she liked how it was growing in, so I kept it. But I'll probably cut it soon.

COLBY. How come? You got dumped?

MARCUS. No, it's not that dramatic. We were just hanging out and I'm going away in the fall, so it's over. Just a little fun, you know? You seeing anybody?

> (**EMMETT** *looks panicked.* **COLBY** *looks at* **MARCUS**, *annoyed.*)

COLBY. Uh...no?

MARCUS. What, too soon?

COLBY. Yeah.

EMMETT. No! It's fine. We're fine.

> (**MARCUS** *studies* **EMMETT**, *who won't meet his gaze.*)

MARCUS. Okay, then.

COLBY. So when did you get home?

MARCUS. Just yesterday.

COLBY. Have you been following the news?

MARCUS. About what?

EMMETT. Colby, help me move this. It's heavy.

COLBY. About what they found behind Forrester Road.

MARCUS. No, what?

EMMETT. Colby.

COLBY. A whole bunch of bodies!

MARCUS. Like, in a pile?

COLBY. No, they were buried in different places all around the woods back there.

MARCUS. You're kidding. Did the cops identify who they were?

COLBY. Not all of 'em. It's a bunch of girls.

MARCUS. Damn, man.

COLBY. They think some might be prostitutes who worked along the expressway. But they're looking into a lot of cold case disappearances.

MARCUS. Right off Forrester?

COLBY. Deeper back into the woods. But yeah.

MARCUS. That's so creepy. It's so close to here.

COLBY. Tell me about it.

MARCUS. Do they know who did it?

EMMETT. They have someone in custody.

COLBY. Your parents haven't said anything about it?

MARCUS. No. Why would they?

COLBY. It was like the first thing my parents said to me when I got home. It's big news in town.

MARCUS. Well, they didn't say anything about it to me.

EMMETT. People in town are kinda freaked out that with all the construction about to start back there they might turn up more.

COLBY. They think this dude's been using it as a dumping ground for years and nobody knew about it.

MARCUS. God, I don't even want to think about it. Can we talk about something else, please?

EMMETT. Yeah, sure.

COLBY. I just thought maybe your mom mentioned it.

MARCUS. Well, she didn't. She knows I don't like stuff like that.

COLBY. I just think it's crazy. You live your whole life some place and the whole time like two miles away there's this mass grave.

MARCUS. Point made, Colby. Can we talk about something less morbid? We're back here for the night, let's make the most of it. Have some fun! Did your mom make brownies?

COLBY. No, I forgot to ask her this year.

MARCUS. Damn, those are the best. So what – it's raw s'mores then for eats?

EMMETT. Hey!

MARCUS. Don't worry. I like marshmallows. That's why I hang around with you two.

COLBY. Ha ha.

EMMETT. You want me to grab you a beer?

MARCUS. Sure.

(**EMMETT** *hands* **MARCUS** *a beer. He opens it and takes a long sip.*)

Mmm. That's better. I did miss you two idiots.

COLBY. Same here, buddy.

(**MARCUS** *toasts his beer to his friends.*)

MARCUS. Here's to the three amigos!

(*Lights dim. The* **BOYS** *set up the sleeping bags and the snacks in a triangle on the floor. In the middle is the board game Life. They sit around the game, several empty beer cans at their sides. Lights restore as the game is almost finished with* **MARCUS** *in the lead. He spins.*)

Scene Two

MARCUS. I'm two spins away from winning, gentlemen.

EMMETT. Only if you get the right spins.

MARCUS. I've been on a hot streak all night. Lady Luck is on my side.

COLBY. This game sucks.

MARCUS. You suck at Life, Colby. Don't hate the players, hate the game.

COLBY. I do hate the game!

EMMETT. You could still catch up.

(**EMMETT** *spins. Moves his car on the board.*)

COLBY. I'm like half the board behind you. I'm screwed.

EMMETT. Yeah, you are. Payday!

(**EMMETT** *and* **MARCUS** *laugh.*)

COLBY. Well, I'm sufficiently buzzed now. Let's talk shit about people.

EMMETT. Ooh, okay!

(**EMMETT** *gets up to get another beer.*)

MARCUS. Finally! I feel like I've been the only one talking this whole time.

COLBY. Can't help it if you love talking about yourself.

MARCUS. Oh, well excuse me!

COLBY. I'm just saying we'd talk if you left us an opening.

EMMETT. Oh, stop sulking about the game. I like your stories, Marcus.

(**EMMETT** *goes to sit down too quickly and bumps the board shifting the pieces. He laughs.)*

COLBY. Are you drunk already?

EMMETT. No! Just excited.

COLBY. Watch what you're doing.

(He resets his piece on the board.)

EMMETT. Um, you were back there!

COLBY. Who cares? I'm still losing.

EMMETT. Well, I'm keeping you honest.

COLBY. Suck a dick.

MARCUS. Okay, are we resettled?

EMMETT. Yes!

MARCUS. Then spill the dirt. What's the gossip on all our good friends who aren't cool enough to be with us tonight?

EMMETT. You assume I know things?

COLBY. We all know you have, like, a pathological need to keep tabs on everybody.

MARCUS. Ten points for "pathological," State School!

COLBY. Oh, whatever. C'mon, Emm. Dish.

MARCUS. Something really good!

EMMETT. Okay. Wendy Marks is pregnant!

COLBY. Get the fuck out.

MARCUS. You're serious?

EMMETT. Five months along. Saw her at CVS yesterday.

COLBY. Wait, how have I not heard this?

EMMETT. She's been intentionally off the grid for a bit.

COLBY. That's insane! Who's the baby daddy?

EMMETT. Don't know.

MARCUS. *You* don't know or *she* doesn't know?

EMMETT. I don't know and I don't know whether or not she knows.

COLBY. You didn't ask her?

EMMETT. I can't ask that!

COLBY. Why not?

EMMETT. Uh, tact?

MARCUS. Well, is she dating anyone?

EMMETT. No. I asked around.

MARCUS. Oh, that's messed up. How'd you keep that to yourself all game?

(**COLBY** *spins and moves.*)

EMMETT. I honestly forgot with everything else going on.

COLBY. Payday!

(**MARCUS** *presents him a card.*)

MARCUS. "Share the wealth."

COLBY. Suck a dick.

(**COLBY** *hands* **MARCUS** *some money.*)

I can't imagine what her dad thinks, that sanctimonious piece of shit.

MARCUS. Another ten points for "sanctimonious," State School!

COLBY. Well, he is! Plus he's the worst teacher we had for all of high school.

EMMETT. Because he lectured you in front of the whole class that time about cheating?

COLBY. Most of that homework was mine! I asked you for like two answers.

EMMETT. Okay, if that's how you remember it.

MARCUS. Hey, anybody hear from Jackson?

(**EMMETT** *spins. Moves his piece.*)

COLBY. YES! You're not going to believe it.

MARCUS. What, he's finally out of the closet?

EMMETT. Yeah. But it's way better than that. He went and got himself a boyfriend!

MARCUS. Okay, so?

EMMETT. He's forty-six years old.

MARCUS. No!

COLBY. Yup, he's an investment banker from Philly. Dude's loaded.

MARCUS. Jackson Porter has a *sugar daddy* – that's what you're telling me?

COLBY. Makes total sense to me.

EMMETT. He told the guy he's twenty-two. They're living together for the summer.

COLBY. No, no! They are *sailing* on the dude's *yacht* together for the summer. Through the *Mediterranean.* That guy's only two years younger than his dad! The best stuff happens to the worst people.

MARCUS. So you're jealous?

COLBY. Fuck, yeah! C'mon, spin. It's your turn. Wait, hold up! How'd you get to the end?

MARCUS. Pay attention! I told you I was right there.

COLBY. No, you moved it when Emm bumped the board!

EMMETT. He did not. He's at the final spin.

MARCUS. C'mon six...

(**MARCUS** *spins.*)

Six! Millionaire Tycoon! I win!

COLBY. You've got to be kidding me.

MARCUS. Spinner landed on my number. Victory is mine!

EMMETT. What can ya do? He gambled. He won.

COLBY. These aren't even the right rules.

EMMETT. Do you want me to read you the rules from the box again?

COLBY. I don't understand what century this game is from. I specifically remember from the version I had that everyone had to finish the game and then we counted the money to see who won.

EMMETT. Considering you didn't even want to play, I'd figure you'd be fine ending the game here.

COLBY. That's not the point.

EMMETT. No, the point is you didn't win. I know.

COLBY. Whatever. Congrats, Millionaire Tycoon. Are you happy we played?

MARCUS. Yeah, I always like this game! You pick next. What do you want to play? Warriors of Catan?

EMMETT. *Settlers* of Catan.

MARCUS. Settlers! My bad.

COLBY. Can we take a rest from board games for a little bit?

(**EMMETT** *gets up.*)

EMMETT. Yeah, I could use a break. Do you want another beer?

COLBY. I'll get it. Winner gets to put the board away.

(**EMMETT** *and* **COLBY** *go to the snacks. As* **MARCUS** *packs the game, he finds a roll of real money in the box. He considers it, hesitates, then pockets it without them noticing.*)

EMMETT. I'm gonna break open these graham crackers.

COLBY. Grab me a couple? And a Hershey's bar.

EMMETT. Here ya go.

(**EMMETT** *passes them to him.* **COLBY** *takes a bite.*)

COLBY. So who else from our class became total screw ups?

EMMETT. Easier to tell you who didn't. Oh! Aaron Brody is in jail again.

COLBY. Again? I thought he just got out.

EMMETT. He did. But he violated parole so he's back in.

MARCUS. Good.

COLBY. What'd he do now?

EMMETT. Hate crime'd two guys in the parking lot of Friday's.

COLBY. Classy. Race hate crime or gay hate crime?

EMMETT. Both kind of? They were Black, and he *thought* they were gay. They weren't, but he didn't really ask for confirmation before he jumped them. Apparently, his hate speech covered all the bases, so take your pick to what his deepest seeded hatred might be.

COLBY. God, when was that kid not a total piece of shit?

MARCUS. Well let's see. It was in fifth grade when he came up to me and told me that my dad got cancer from having to look at my ugly face everyday. And that was the week after he died, so...

EMMETT. Yeah, he's always been the worst.

COLBY. Alright, I'm done talking about Aaron fucking Brody. New rule: From here on out we only gossip about people we actually care about.

EMMETT. Agreed.

> (**EMMETT** *eyes the game box.*)

Can I take that from you?

MARCUS. Hmm?

EMMETT. I'll put it back over there.

> (**MARCUS** *hands* **EMMETT** *the box. He brings it back to the table.*)

MARCUS. Hey, have either of you heard from Angela lately?

COLBY. Angela *Bercy*? No, I don't ever talk to her.

EMMETT. Just posts online. Why?

MARCUS. Do you know if she's seeing someone?

EMMETT. Um, yeah. I think so. I saw some pictures of her at college with some guy. But I mean, I don't know if it's serious. Would that be a problem for you if it was?

MARCUS. No, it's just that I think she blocked me online. I tried to tag her in a post last week about coming home and I couldn't do it and then I realized I couldn't see her profile. Then I noticed all her pages online were blocked from me. And I didn't know why she'd do that.

> (**EMMETT** *and* **COLBY** *consult each other with a look.*)

COLBY. She hasn't come up in my news feed in a while, now that you mention it. Maybe she did a friend purge this spring.

MARCUS. Yeah, but why?

EMMETT. Well, maybe she is dating someone new and she'd rather cut ties with her exes. Some people are weird like that. And maybe she just thinks Colby is a loser.

COLBY. People do tend to reach that conclusion over time.

MARCUS. I guess. I thought we were in a better place. We never even dated that seriously. It wasn't anything like you guys had. You split up, but you didn't cut each other out of your lives.

EMMETT. To be fair, we did at the beginning, Marcus. I blocked Colby for a while.

COLBY. You did?

EMMETT. Fuck yeah, I did. For like three months or something. I didn't need to see whatever you were up to right at the beginning.

MARCUS. Fine, but you're here together now. I just don't understand why she suddenly decides, "I don't want to have anything to do with Marcus." I never did anything bad to her.

COLBY. Why stress over it? We don't have to stay friends with every person we grew up with.

MARCUS. She was my first kiss, dude.

COLBY. We *know*.

MARCUS. Sixth grade in the woods behind Forrester Road – oh man that's so creepy now!

EMMETT. Mmhmm.

MARCUS. Now when I think about all the times we hung out back there, I'm gonna think we were probably running around on top of dead bodies.

(**MARCUS** *does a body shiver. Drinks more of the beer.*)

EMMETT. It's not right off Forrester. It's further back. We wouldn't have played back there. You hungry? I've got lots of snacks.

MARCUS. Not right now. I'm so bummed the TV's gone. What happened to it?

(**EMMETT** *starts to answer when something clicks in* **MARCUS**' *head.*)

Oh wait! The hurricane, right?

EMMETT. Yeah. Tree fell and busted in the side over there. Lots of rain came in. Ruined a lot of stuff, the biggest casualty being the TV.

MARCUS. R.I.P. TV. *That's* what looks different outside. That tree's missing.

EMMETT. Yeah. You can see over there that wood's all new.

MARCUS. Oh yeah. Did you lose a lot of other stuff?

EMMETT. My dad lost some prints. I lost a box of comics and some photo albums.

(**COLBY** *looks at* **EMMETT** *with raised concern.*)

COLBY. The scrapbook?

EMMETT. No, I have it. I never stored that out here.

COLBY. Okay. But you brought it –

EMMETT. Yeah, I have it for later.

MARCUS. I was really jonesing for some *Smash Bros. MELEE!*

COLBY. I know. I wanted to play *Mario Kart.*

MARCUS. You suck at *Mario Kart.*

COLBY. I do not. We used to kill it together on two player.

MARCUS. Well, yeah, when I was driving and you were in the back punching people. Then we dominated.

COLBY. Diddy and Koopa! Rock solid.

EMMETT. Diddy and Koopa were little punks.

COLBY. Just 'cause you always had to be Peach.

EMMETT. I wasn't always Peach.

MARCUS. You were always Peach. And Dustin Davies was Mario. Remember when you had that huge crush on Dustin Davies and he had no idea?

EMMETT. I didn't have a –

MARCUS. Don't even lie.

COLBY. You did!

EMMETT. Where do you get "huge crush"? I just thought he was cool.

COLBY. Revisionist history. He was over here all the time before his family moved.

EMMETT. Yeah, in seventh grade!

MARCUS. Do you know what happened to him?

COLBY. I think he goes to Maryland now.

EMMETT. No, not Maryland. He's at William and Mary!

COLBY. I stand corrected. Remember that time Emmett asked Dustin if he wanted to watch *Titanic*?

(**COLBY** *and* **MARCUS** *laugh.*)

EMMETT. You guys are assholes.

COLBY. *(As young Emmett.)* Hey guys, my dad just got the Special Edition of *Titanic* on DVD, you wanna watch? It's got great commentaries. What do you say, Dustin?

MARCUS. *(As Dustin.)* Uh, no?

(They laugh again.)

EMMETT. Whatever. I wasn't like that.

MARCUS. Hey, it's okay to own it. You liked Dustin. You liked being Peach to his Mario. You liked *Titanic*. Look how far you've come from that time.

EMMETT. You can shut up now.

COLBY. You liked being Peach in *Smash Bros.* too!

EMMETT. No.

MARCUS. Yeah, you liked to play Peach, Samus, Zelda and Jigglypuff.

COLBY. Surprise! You liked being all the girls.

EMMETT. Jigglypuff's not necessarily a girl.

COLBY. She is too!

EMMETT. No, in Pokémon, there are both male and female Jigglypuff. Females are more common but in *Smash Brothers* they always refer to Jiggly as "it."

MARCUS. Nerd Academy is correct.

COLBY. It's a girl character.

EMMETT. Why?

COLBY. She's pink!

MARCUS. Man, I hope you've signed up for a Gender Studies elective for the fall semester. You need to educate yourself.

EMMETT. Colby's just talking out of his ass again.

MARCUS. Man, *Melee* was the best. All the *Smash Brothers* are the best. I used to have the original for the N64 too. What did I do with that thing?

COLBY. I'm pretty sure you put it in the time capsule!

EMMETT. Really, Colby?

MARCUS. Oh my god, the time capsule! That thing's still under here, isn't it?

COLBY. Yeah, Emmett and I were talking about it before you got here.

MARCUS. You are never gonna let us dig that thing up, huh?

EMMETT. My dad doesn't want / anyone going under there.

COLBY. It's not that your dad doesn't want you to dig it up. You don't want to dig it up.

EMMETT. So what?

COLBY. So you said you would when we turned sixteen.

EMMETT. I think my exact phrasing was "after we're sixteen" not immediately upon turning sixteen, so it's not a broken promise. It's just one that's yet-to-be-fulfilled.

MARCUS. Man, I did put that in the time capsule. Why did I do that?

COLBY. Because it wasn't supposed to be down there forever.

EMMETT. Well, that's how things work out sometimes.

MARCUS. I don't remember what else I put in there. It must've been like toys and stuff, right?

COLBY. Yeah and then Emmett made us write letters to ourselves.

MARCUS. Yes, you did!

COLBY. Do you remember what you wrote?

MARCUS. No idea. I'm sure it was really deep thirteen-year-old stuff. You?

COLBY. I don't think I wrote anything.

EMMETT. Yes, you did. We all did.

COLBY. Well, we could dig it up now and see.

EMMETT. How many times / do I have to say no?

COLBY. Fine! How about we play one of your stupid board games then, Emmett.

MARCUS. Hey, chill out, Colby. Don't be a dick.

COLBY. I'm not being a dick.

MARCUS. Well, have another beer and relax.

EMMETT. I guess I should've figured out a way to bring the TV / out here from the house.

COLBY. No, it's just / we're only delaying the inevitable. I mean what's the point in –

EMMETT. Hell, you didn't even want to stay originally / and I know you're trying to –

MARCUS. You didn't want to stay?

COLBY. I thought it'd be weird to have a sleepover with just my ex-boyfriend if you didn't show.

MARCUS. Why wouldn't I show? You said that earlier too. Do you think I'm that unreliable / that I wouldn't show? Because I pride myself on being a dependable person.

COLBY. No, you're very reliable. It's just that there's a lot that's going on recently and I didn't know if that would affect –

MARCUS. Nothing's going on with me.

COLBY. Things are going on, Marcus. They are.

MARCUS. What is he talking about?

EMMETT. We're doing this now?

COLBY. Yes, now Emmett.

MARCUS. Guys.

EMMETT. There are some things we want to talk to you about, Marcus. Recent developments.

MARCUS. Regarding what?

EMMETT. Regarding your family.

MARCUS. What about them? They're fine.

EMMETT. They're really kinda not, buddy. And I know you know that.

MARCUS. Somebody explain to me what's going on. Right now.

COLBY. Why do we have these sleepovers, Marcus?

MARCUS. Believe me. I'm seriously asking myself that question right now.

COLBY. No, for real. There's a reason. What's the reason?

MARCUS. Because it's tradition. This is what we always do.

EMMETT. What's the tradition?

MARCUS. Start of summer sleepover. Since we were thirteen.

COLBY. Why today?

MARCUS. Because that's when we buried the time capsule.

COLBY. No, that's not the right day. We did that in the fall the year before.

MARCUS. Guys, I don't remember then. Just tell me.

COLBY. It has to do with Man Hunt.

MARCUS. Oh! Yeah! That was the big Man Hunt game. With the whole neighborhood.

EMMETT. That's right.

MARCUS. And we were all on the same team, as always.

EMMETT. Correct.

COLBY. You remember where we hid?

MARCUS. I dunno. All over the place. No. Wait. The Dungeon, right?

EMMETT. No, not that night. We wouldn't all fit.

MARCUS. That's right. So we climbed on the roof of Mr. McLellan's shed!

COLBY. No.

MARCUS. Yes, we did! I remember now.

EMMETT. No, that's where Colby and I hid, Marcus.

COLBY. Eventually. First we all went –

MARCUS. Up behind Forrester Road. That was it!

(*A wave of memories floods over him.*)

Oh...

COLBY. Yeah. And you know what happened then?

MARCUS. I ditched you. Emmett wanted to go back, so I ditched you. I kept going.

EMMETT. That's right. And then?

MARCUS. I got tired and I came back here to sleep.

COLBY. No, you didn't.

MARCUS. (*He reconsiders.*) No. I just went home. And nobody knew where I was and you all got really worried!

EMMETT. No, Marcus. You didn't go home either.

MARCUS. No... I didn't come back here. And I didn't go home. And nobody knew where I was and everyone got really worried.

(*He thinks hard. He figures it out.*)

I never came home, did I?

EMMETT. No, you didn't.

MARCUS. Where did I go?

EMMETT. We wish we knew, buddy.

MARCUS. *(Realizations start to come more quickly.)* I went missing. I'm still missing, aren't I? I'm lost? I'm lost? I don't...

EMMETT. I'm so sorry, Marcus.

(**MARCUS** *retreats. He shudders and whimpers.*)

You're here with us. You're okay.

MARCUS. But that can't be right. I remember going to school with you guys. Graduation. College. All the crazy shit we did together.

COLBY. You weren't there for that stuff. You didn't go to prom. You just fill in the gaps for yourself.

MARCUS. But I knew about your play!

EMMETT. Yeah, you have a funny way of doing that. You can pull stuff out of us. You insert yourself into things that happened, but you weren't there.

MARCUS. But the sleepovers. Those happened. I was here for those.

EMMETT. You were. Those did happen. Every year on the day you disappeared. Those memories are real.

COLBY. We freaked out pretty majorly that first year you showed, remember?

EMMETT. We were thrilled, actually. We thought you were finally home.

COLBY. But it became clear really fast it wasn't really you.

EMMETT. No, he means it was *you*. Of course it was. You were a year older. Taller. But –

COLBY. You weren't abused. You were fine.

EMMETT. You didn't look like you'd been living in the woods for a year. And you acted like –

COLBY. You just started talking to us as if nothing happened. Which pissed us off, obviously. We kept screaming you had to go see your mom. We were practically on the floor crying.

EMMETT. And then you remembered. You said you couldn't go back home. You could only come here to see us and you'd be gone before morning.

MARCUS. Oh. Yeah. That's right.

COLBY. We do this every year, Marcus. You come, and you go, and you don't leave anything behind.

MARCUS. What do you mean?

COLBY. I mean we've tried everything to keep some trace of you here. You don't show up in pictures or video. Your voice doesn't record. Our phones don't carry a signal.

EMMETT. We tried having you write letters. We even had you write in a Sharpie on the wall over there. You leave and it vanishes. So after the first two years we just decided to stop trying and enjoy the time you were around.

COLBY. You asked us to stop trying.

MARCUS. Yeah... you think I'd be able to remember that.

EMMETT. We started the scrapbook to help you keep track of everything.

> (*He goes to get a large scrapbook out of a backpack.*)

There's newspaper stories in here and pictures of people and things.

MARCUS. Every year I come back and you're waiting for me.

COLBY. That's right.

MARCUS. We get to share the night together. I remember now. I'm so glad you guys are here with me.

EMMETT. We are too, Marcus. We really are.

MARCUS. No... Colby thought I wouldn't come this year. Because of the bodies, right?

COLBY. Yeah, because of the bodies.

MARCUS. But they didn't find my body.

EMMETT. So far it's only girls. No boys.

(**MARCUS** *turns a page and stares at it.*)

MARCUS. Who's this?

EMMETT. That's James Bernard Kasperak.

COLBY. Do you know him?

MARCUS. I don't think so. Should I?

EMMETT. He's the guy they have in custody for the other murders. About six weeks ago he picked up a girl along the expressway, meaning to kill her, but she was able to fight him off and she got away. The police tracked him down and arrested him.

MARCUS. Whoa. I'm glad she escaped.

COLBY. Yeah, well it wasn't the cleanest getaway.

EMMETT. Colby.

COLBY. It wasn't! I read that article too. It says it right in there.

EMMETT. The point is: they checked his house and... *found things* and then searched the area near to where the girl was on the expressway and then the search area expanded.

COLBY. And they found the bodies buried behind Forrester Road.

MARCUS. He lives around here?

EMMETT. Like an hour or so away.

COLBY. He lived closer a few years ago. He was definitely in the area around the time you disappeared.

MARCUS. And they think he's responsible for whatever happened to me?

COLBY. Yes.

EMMETT. Not everyone is so sure.

COLBY. He is claiming responsibility though.

EMMETT. Your family says that he says he did it, but the police can't find your body out there and Kasperak hasn't been able to give them details yet like he has for some of the girls.

MARCUS. So you think he could be lying? Why would he lie?

COLBY. Why would he kill people? He's obviously a sick individual. Who knows what his motives are?

EMMETT. That's why we want to talk to you about it. Whether or not you remember him could bring a lot of people closure. Or at least stop your folks from following another false lead.

COLBY. So what do you say?

(**MARCUS** *stares at the picture.*)

EMMETT. Is this guy familiar to you at all?

MARCUS. No. I don't know. I can't remember.

COLBY. Well, think about it, Marcus!

MARCUS. I am thinking about it!

COLBY. No, you're not! I can see in your face you're resisting going back there.

MARCUS. No, I'm trying to concentrate! I'm focusing.

EMMETT. Attacking him's not gonna make it easier.

MARCUS. Guys, I am sorry you have to go through this, and I am sorry that I can't be of more help. But look at this thing.

(*He pages through the scrapbook.*)

You guys are bigger experts on the subject than I am. I only know what I know. I wish I could give you the answers. If the facts are somewhere in my brain, I wish I could get to them, but I don't know how to do it. Was this guy involved? Was he not involved? I don't know. I just can't give you what you're looking for.

(**COLBY** *bites his lip and turns away from them.*)

EMMETT. It's okay. We've still got a lot of time left tonight and sometimes, as it gets later, you have a better sense –

MARCUS. I don't want to think about it anymore. Tonight's supposed to be a gift for us to share together. I get to enjoy one happy night the whole year where I'm fine and everything's normal and we're just hanging out together.

EMMETT. Yeah, and usually we're fine to do that, but if we could do this first –

MARCUS. But I can't do it, Emm. You don't understand how hard it is to just –

COLBY. We don't understand how hard it is?

MARCUS. No, that's not what I was / trying to say. I meant that it's hard –

COLBY. Do you have any idea what we've been going through? What your family goes through every day? It's been killing them slowly for six years. And here you are telling us you won't even try to think about it because it's too hard? Because you want to have a nice night? Fuck you. Tell us what we need to know and then maybe we'll go back to the fucking board games.

EMMETT. Colby, shut up!

COLBY. No, Emmett! I won't! This is bullshit.

MARCUS. Colby, I was just trying to say that it's hard for me to trust what's in my head, okay? You tell me I've been gone and I know that's true, but at the same time I have this other history in my head of all these memories where we've been together and it's not so easy to just separate them and tell you what's real. They're both real for me.

COLBY. None of this is right. You just shouldn't be here.

MARCUS. Okay, but I am here.

COLBY. Why? What are you?

MARCUS. I'm your friend, Colby.

COLBY. No, you're not. My friend Marcus disappeared when he was thirteen and whatever you are, you obviously don't want any part in us figuring out what really happened to him. Maybe you're some kind of changeling. Maybe you killed him and take his shape once a year. I don't know. Who knows what kind of stuff is out there in the woods?

EMMETT. Colby, what the hell is going on with you?

COLBY. God, Emmett. You're such an idiot. This is not Marcus. It's not his ghost. Ghosts don't grow up. They don't drink beer and play games and ask you to bake them fucking brownies. Touch him!

> (**COLBY** *grabs* **MARCUS**' *arm.* **MARCUS** *twists away.*)

He's warm. He's alive!

EMMETT. That's enough! If you want to leave so badly /
that you would start talking to him like –

MARCUS. No! No, he can't leave.

COLBY. Why not? I can go if I want. You two hang out
together. Pretend reality is whatever you want it to be.

MARCUS. You can't go. It has to be the three of us.

COLBY. Why? Why us?

MARCUS. That's just how it is. I couldn't be here if it was
any more or any less than the three of us.

COLBY. And how do you know that?

MARCUS. I just do. I *feel* it. You think I don't want to see
my family? I want it so much! But you'd bring them
here and I'd be gone and then what would that do to
them?

COLBY. You never even let us try! We could just bring
your mom. We are not the people who need the gift of
seeing you once a year, Marcus! She is! It's not fair! We
can't go on just keeping this a secret. It's wrong.

MARCUS. I didn't make the rules, okay? I didn't ask for this.

COLBY. Who makes the rules then, Marcus? Who calls the
shots?

MARCUS. I. Don't. Know.

COLBY. Well, then what are the rules exactly? You come
back for one night with a bunch of memories of things
that never happened. You can't remember the truth
until you suddenly do remember the truth, but then
you still can't tell us any details about what happened
to you that night. You can only show up if it's just the
three or us and if we bring anyone else to see you, you
might disappear forever. Does that sum it up?

MARCUS. Why are you attacking me?

COLBY. Because look at us. We're not little kids anymore. And it was wrong to tell us back then to keep this secret for you. That's what abusers do.

EMMETT. I cannot believe you just said that.

COLBY. It's true! Emmett, you're so wrapped up in the "bond" aspect of this that you're not looking at what's going on here. He's never going to help us solve the mystery of where Marcus went. This *thing* is not interested in that.

MARCUS. I'm not a thing! Don't talk to me like that!

COLBY. Marcus should want us to tell. He should want people to know he's alive or dead or lost or whatever. He shouldn't want to just shoot the breeze with us for a night before disappearing again.

EMMETT. Why not? If that's all I could get, I would take it.

COLBY. And what are we supposed to do? Just keep coming back here every year for the rest of our lives so that "Marcus" gets his day in the land of the living?

EMMETT. That's our responsibility.

COLBY. Until when? We're going to still be doing this in our forties? What if your parents sell your house and move someplace else? This is not a sustainable plan. And you're not an idiot so I wish you would understand that and face reality.

EMMETT. The reality I'm facing is that my friend is standing in front of me and he needs my support. So I'm going to be here for him. Maybe it's easier for you to turn your back, I don't know –

COLBY. Turn my back?

EMMETT. I don't know.

COLBY. Don't turn this into being about me and you, Emmett.

EMMETT. I wasn't –

COLBY. You totally are doing that! You're trying to hold on to Marcus as a way of holding on to us. To the relationship –

EMMETT. Not everything in my life is about you, Colby!

COLBY. It sure used to be.

EMMETT. Well, it's not anymore. Your message was received in January. Believe me.

MARCUS. You don't have to do things this way, Colby.

COLBY. I'm just so tired of it, Marcus. God, I don't even want to call you that and I'm doing it anyway. It's like I'm under some spell or something.

MARCUS. Why are you being this way? You've always accepted me for who I am. Why is it different now?

COLBY. Because it is. I've been seeing someone.

MARCUS. Like...dating?

COLBY. No, not like dating. At school this year, I've been going to a therapist at the mental health office.

EMMETT. Why?

COLBY. Because I had stuff to talk about! This is not possible, it's not normal and I needed –

EMMETT. We already went to counseling.

COLBY. When we were kids, Emm. It wasn't –

MARCUS. You told this person about me.

COLBY. Stop looking in my head! But yeah, I did.

EMMETT. Colby!

COLBY. I had to! I had all this stuff I was feeling about it and I've never talked about it!

EMMETT. We have so talked about it!

COLBY. But I can't just talk about it with you. It's not the same!

EMMETT. So this person's the one who's been telling you Marcus isn't real. That none of this is, right?

COLBY. Yeah.

EMMETT. Well, how the fuck would they know, being outside of it? This is special, Colby. It's magical.

COLBY. Is it, Emmett? Maybe it's just messed up. Maybe it's dangerous. I don't know.

MARCUS. You think I'm putting you in danger?

COLBY. I'm not the bad guy here, Marcus.

MARCUS. I'm not saying you're the bad guy! There is no bad guy!

COLBY. There is! James Bernard Kasperak is a bad guy. But is he our bad guy? Is he yours? I don't know! Can you please just tell us so we know?

MARCUS. I am not hiding things from you. I can't tell you what I don't know!

COLBY. Where do you go when you're not here, Marcus? Do you know that? When you visit me in my dreams is that really you visiting me, or is that just happening in my head? I don't know what you're capable of. Because I have this one dream where it really feels like it's you and you take me into the woods behind Forrester and you show me this one tree that's back there and you say "Here I am, Colby. If you dig between these two giant roots, you'll find my body. You can take me to my parents and I'll be at rest. Please, Colby. Do it for me." Is that you, Marcus?

EMMETT. You never told me you dreamed that.

COLBY. It's happened a bunch. And every time, I go out the next day, take a shovel from the garage and head out there looking for that tree in the woods. I spent a whole day out there once, just thinking if I found my way to that tree, I could find you and I would set you free. But that tree isn't out there, Marcus. It's not out there and I don't know where you are. I can't find you! I just want to find you. Can't you understand?

MARCUS. I'm right here, Colby.

COLBY. You shouldn't be.

MARCUS. But I am.

COLBY. I hate you.

MARCUS. Okay, if you think I deserve that.

COLBY. Shut up. I don't need... I want you both to know that I'm leaving and I'm not coming back. I couldn't anyway if I wanted to. The truth is my parents are selling our house and we're moving away, so this is really the last time I'll be back here.

EMMETT. What are you talking about?

COLBY. They're moving, okay?

EMMETT. Where?

COLBY. Virginia Beach. At the end of the summer.

EMMETT. You're lying.

COLBY. Believe what you want. I'm not coming back here again. So if he wants to admit to what he is or wants to tell us what really happened that night, this is his last chance. Because you and me coming back to this place for him again is not gonna happen.

EMMETT. You have no right to do this. To just dump this on me –

MARCUS. It's okay, Emmett. Colby, you should go if you want to go.

EMMETT. No!

MARCUS. It's obvious I'm hurting you guys. Both of you. I thought... Look, I don't know where I go when I'm not here, but I haven't really been thinking about where you go either. You have to live in a world without me, with people who miss me. And you miss me. You spend the whole rest of the year wondering and looking for clues, hoping for answers. And I come in with this version of things where none of that happens and you play along on my behalf. But it's hurting you. Maybe we should just say goodbye tonight.

COLBY. Is that some kind of reverse psychology move?

MARCUS. It makes it easier on you to think I'm some sinister being, huh Colbs? That I'm some creature pretending to be your friend? It's easier to cut ties with a monster?

(**COLBY** *turns away from* **MARCUS.**)

COLBY. Emmett, I gotta get out of here.

(**COLBY** *goes to exit.*)

EMMETT. We're not done here.

COLBY. I say we are. There's nothing left here that I want to go through again.

EMMETT. There's the time capsule.

COLBY. Whatever we put in there is just a bunch of junk you want to keep buried out in your yard, so, fine.

EMMETT. That's not where the time capsule is anymore.

COLBY. What do you mean? Where is it?

(**MARCUS** *stares at* **EMMETT.**)

MARCUS. You dug it up.

(**EMMETT** *doesn't respond.*)

COLBY. You did?

EMMETT. Yeah, I did. It's in that trunk over there underneath the boxes.

COLBY. But you always said – when did you –

EMMETT. When my dad was fixing the wall over spring break he had to pull out the tree. It left a hole and I crawled down into the Dungeon and dug it out.

COLBY. Did you open it?

EMMETT. No, I didn't open it! I wasn't sure I was even going to tell you I dug it up. I definitely wasn't going to open it without the three of us being together. But if you're going to go, Colby, you at least owe it to us to stay and open it first.

COLBY. It's just stuff. It doesn't matter.

EMMETT. It does matter. You can go and move on and do whatever the fuck you want, but first you're gonna do this with us. If it's goodbye, after everything we've been through, let's lay it all out there.

MARCUS. Let's do it.

COLBY. You want to look through it?

MARCUS. Hell, yeah. I want to see what's inside. You do too. You've been wanting to open it since the day we buried it. So…?

COLBY. Fine. I'm in. But then that's the end of it.

EMMETT. Fine. Help me get it out.

> (**MARCUS** and **COLBY** *help* **EMMETT** *remove the boxes on top of the trunk and drag it more centrally into the room.* **EMMETT** *opens it. The* **BOYS** *look inside skeptically.*)

COLBY. It's dirty.

EMMETT. Well, it was buried underground.

COLBY. You didn't think to, like, rinse it off?

EMMETT. No, I didn't.

MARCUS. Do you have a towel or something? We could wipe it down.

EMMETT. There's cleaning stuff back there.

(*He goes to get a towel.*)

MARCUS. It's bigger than I remembered it.

COLBY. That's what he said.

EMMETT. Really, Colby?

COLBY. Do you have scissors or a knife? How are we gonna get through that duct tape?

> (**EMMETT** *goes to the table with the snacks and gets a knife and brings it back.* **COLBY** *lifts the time capsule out of the trunk. It's a cylindrical waste basket that says "Penn State" on the side, with duct tape wrapped around a makeshift lid.*)

Why did we go to town on it with the tape?

> (**COLBY** *places the can on the floor.*)

EMMETT. You did that. It didn't have a lid that fit so you sealed it.

MARCUS. Yeah, that was all you.

COLBY. Whatever. Gimme. I'll get it off.

> (*He takes the knife and begins cutting through.*)

MARCUS. That was my can, huh? My mom got it for me. Penn State.

EMMETT. Yeah, you liked it even back then.

MARCUS. She got it 'cause my dad went there. And then I put it in the ground. She must've been thrilled.

EMMETT. You told her –

MARCUS. That I was keeping it in the clubhouse. That's right. I lied.

COLBY. Well, it was under the Clubhouse. It wasn't a total lie.

MARCUS. It held up pretty well!

EMMETT. Yeah, it's still intact. You're sure you want to open it?

COLBY. Yes. Don't you want to still open it?

EMMETT. Don't yell at me, Colby. / I'm just making sure you really want to do it before it's done.

COLBY. I'm not yelling at you, we just already agreed to it, so stop asking.

MARCUS. Let's just do it.

(**MARCUS** *bends down and pulls at the tape. He recoils as if his hand is scalded.* **EMMETT** *and* **COLBY** *shout in concern.*)

EMMETT. Marcus!

(**MARCUS** *laughs and shows them he's fine.*)

MARCUS. I'm sorry. I couldn't resist.

EMMETT. That's not funny.

MARCUS. I was just trying to lighten the mood.

COLBY. Okay, it was a little funny.

(*They all chuckle.*)

EMMETT. Seriously, did you feel anything?

MARCUS. No. Let's keep going. Let's open it. I don't think it's going to do what you think it's going to do.

(*They all work on removing the tape.*)

EMMETT. What do you think I think it's gonna do?

MARCUS. You're looking at me like some ball of light is gonna burst out of me until I burn up and disappear. I'm not Freddy Krueger.

COLBY. Okay, it's off.

EMMETT. Alright, just open it.

(**MARCUS** *makes a kazoo noise.* **COLBY** *opens the lid.* **EMMETT** *and* **COLBY** *look inside. They both look back up at* **MARCUS** *to see if he's still there.*)

MARCUS. Still here, guys. Empty it out. Let's see what we got.

(**EMMETT** *picks up a paper from the can and reads it.*)

EMMETT. "TIME CAPSULE – buried on November 16, 2008. Not to be unearthed before November 16, 2011 and with all parties present: Emmett Sheffield, Colby Gustafson, and Marcus Jones." And we all signed it.

COLBY. You were very formal back then, Emm.

EMMETT. Apparently.

(**COLBY** *looks through the bin.*)

COLBY. I forgot you bagged and labeled everything! Here, Marcus!

(**COLBY** *tosses him a bag with a game cartridge.*)

MARCUS. *Smash Bros*!

COLBY. All these bags...

EMMETT. I wanted to make sure the dirt didn't get in. This one has your name on it too, Marcus.

> (*He tosses him the bag.* **COLBY** *picks up one with a VHS tape.*)

COLBY. *The Three Amigos*! On VHS? When did we have a VCR out here?

EMMETT. We didn't. That was my dad's old copy. He didn't need it anymore.

MARCUS. God, Emm, we watched that so many times.

> (**COLBY** *puts it down and opens a bag filled with magazine clippings of movie characters. He looks through them.*)

COLBY. What is this stuff? Wall-E... The Joker... Iron Man...

EMMETT. That's mine! I cut those out of Entertainment Weekly. That's what came out that year.

COLBY. *Mamma Mia*?

> (**COLBY** *laughs.*)

Only thirteen-year-old you would save magazine ads of *Mamma Mia*!

EMMETT. You liked that movie!

COLBY. I did not! You liked it. Ooh, *Kung Fu Panda*! I loved *Kung Fu Panda*.

MARCUS. That was quality.

> (**EMMETT** *tries to hand* **COLBY** *a different bag.*)

EMMETT. Here. This is your bag. It has your name on it.

COLBY. Okay, but what else is in here?

EMMETT. I don't know. I'm looking through it.

COLBY. Bionicles... why'd you put these in here?

EMMETT. They were broken. We were burying them.

COLBY. Oh. And that's all that's in here?

EMMETT. Look at your own stuff!

COLBY. Fine! What's in your bag, Marcus?

MARCUS. Look.

(*He shows* **COLBY** *a Polaroid.*)

COLBY. Oh man, who took this?

MARCUS. Emmett's dad. At his thirteenth birthday party.

EMMETT. Who's in it?

COLBY. It's Marcus and Angela Bercy. You *did* have a thing for her.

MARCUS. Here's my seventh grade soccer medal. My JV pin. And last but not least – my kazoo!

(*He blows on it.*)

COLBY. Okay, now I'm remembering why we made you bury that thing.

MARCUS. What's in your bag?

COLBY. Nothing! A pair of socks.

EMMETT. Why did you put those socks in there?

COLBY. I don't know. In case I needed a clean pair in the future. These are good socks.

(*He unravels them. Cards fall to the floor.*)

EMMETT. What are these?

COLBY. Oh...

(**EMMETT** *examines them. They are Pokémon cards.*)

EMMETT. Infernape? Regigigas? Torterra? These are my Pokémon cards! And this is Marcus' school ID.

MARCUS. What?

EMMETT. I thought I lost those. Why are they in your socks?

COLBY. I guess I hid them there?

EMMETT. I was convinced my cousin stole them from me over Thanksgiving that year! I've been accusing her for six years of messing up my Diamond and Pearl deck.

COLBY. Okay, so this year you can apologize to her for that.

MARCUS. Why do you have my school ID?

COLBY. I don't know! Look how funny your hair looks in the picture!

MARCUS. I had to pay for a new one.

COLBY. Oh, what, like two bucks?

MARCUS. Five bucks.

COLBY. Okay, so I'll give you five bucks. I hope it comes in handy when you go back to wherever you are the rest of the year.

EMMETT. Colby, why did you hide this stuff in your socks?

COLBY. Who knows? Obviously I didn't remember doing it, otherwise I wouldn't have rolled them out like that. I probably thought it'd be funny – that we'd open it up and I'd be like "Surprise! Here's your stuff you thought you lost!" I don't know. I was an idiot.

EMMETT. I made a big deal about the cards being gone. They were from the Stormfront expansion that was brand new.

COLBY. I didn't even know what you were talking about. Come on, you are getting upset over nothing. Over three stupid cards!

MARCUS. And my ID.

COLBY. Fine. Four stupid cards. It was a million years ago! Is there anything else in there?

EMMETT. The Bionicles.

COLBY. Did we really play with Bionicles in Junior High?

MARCUS. No, we broke them in Junior High.

COLBY. We had like an army of them at one point.

EMMETT. Yeah, not anymore.

(**MARCUS** *examines one of the Bionicles.*)

MARCUS. What was this one called?

EMMETT. Its real name? I don't know.

MARCUS. No, what you called it.

EMMETT. Oh. Gravasticore.

(**COLBY** *picks up another one from the bin.*)

MARCUS. Yeah! And that one?

EMMETT. Cymballistix.

COLBY. Where did you come up with this shit?

EMMETT. I don't know. TV shows and stuff.

MARCUS. No, you'd ramble on for hours about these guys. These were the kings, right?

EMMETT. Yeah, they each ruled their own universe and they sent armies to attack each other through wormholes.

COLBY. And we buried them together. That was nice of us.

EMMETT. Well, they were also brothers.

COLBY. Oh, yeah! There was a whole family.

EMMETT. And they were the last survivors.

(**MARCUS** *turns away looking for something in the bags on the floor.* **COLBY** *considers* **EMMETT** *for a moment.*)

COLBY. Hey.

EMMETT. What?

COLBY. I'm sorry. I mean it. Okay?

(**EMMETT** *considers this silently.*)

MARCUS. That can't be everything. My letter's missing.

COLBY. Oh, mine too, I guess.

EMMETT. They're all in here. I put them in a separate bag.

MARCUS. Well, hand 'em out. Let's read.

EMMETT. I'm not in the mood to read mine now.

COLBY. Then I'll read it.

EMMETT. Why should you read it?

MARCUS. Yes! That's what we'll do. We'll all read someone else's. Out loud. No edits. Whatever was written, we say it out loud.

COLBY. Wait, I don't even know what I said.

EMMETT. Okay. I'll do it.

COLBY. Can we look at it first?

EMMETT. No.

MARCUS. Who reads whose?

EMMETT. Marcus, you read Colby's. I'll read yours. He can read mine.

COLBY. Do you know what you wrote?

EMMETT. Basically. I dunno. I'm not afraid to hear it though.

COLBY. Fine. Hand it over.

(**EMMETT** *hands out the letters. They have been folded into triangles. They all unwrap the letters.*)

MARCUS. Whose letter's first?

COLBY. Do you want to hear yours?

MARCUS. No, not first.

COLBY. How about I read Emmett's then?

EMMETT. Fine with me. Go for it.

COLBY. Okay, from the pen of thirteen-year-old Emmett.

(*He reads off the paper.*)

"Dear Self,

"Hey! I convinced the guys to write letters to our future selves for the time capsule, and now I have no idea what I want to write. I should write something important since it was my idea, but now that I'm sitting here, I don't know!"

– this is great so far, Emm –

"We're in the clubhouse. Colby is sitting on my left and he's writing away really fast and he has a stupid grin on his face so I know he's not writing anything important. Marcus looks like he's thinking. He's definitely putting thought into it. He's a good writer too. I have to come up with something good.

"It's three years from now. What do I want to have happen in three years? OH MY GOD – *LOST*!"

– that part is all in caps –

"OH MY GOD – *LOST*! You will know the ending of *Lost*. Unless it's still going. No, it can't still be going. I mean, it could. But it can't. I don't want it to. You, future self, know the ending, and all the mysteries of the island are solved, and I am jealous of you for knowing while I still have to wait it out."

– So young and naive we were. –

EMMETT. Let's not even go there now. Just keep reading.

COLBY. "In three years, I hope I smell better."

EMMETT. What?

COLBY. That's what it says.

EMMETT. I didn't write that!

COLBY. You did. Will you let me finish?

MARCUS. Emm, whatever's there, just laugh at it now.

EMMETT. How much is left?

COLBY. A couple more lines.

EMMETT. Fine.

COLBY. "In three years, I hope I smell better. PLEASE GOD. This is embarrassing to admit, but I guess I'm just admitting it to myself, but I know I don't smell good. And you know that I shower all the time but I can't get the smell off. Dad says it's just puberty, so I hope in three years that this part of puberty is OVER. I'd rather have a face full of acne like Jamie and smell good, than have a cute face and stink."

EMMETT. Which basically happened two years later, so I guess I got what I wished for.

COLBY. Hold on this is the best part. "Dustin is never gonna date me if I stink! Also, please let Dustin decide that he's gay. That'd be awesome."

(**COLBY** and **MARCUS** burst out laughing.)

EMMETT. You guys – shut up! I cannot wait to read what you all wrote.

COLBY. I told you. You loved him!

EMMETT. It wasn't –

MARCUS. Dude, you wrote it down. Stop denying.

EMMETT. Is there more?

COLBY. Just a little. "My page is full! Did I say anything? Get good grades so you can go to a good college. Don't drink. Don't smoke. Don't do drugs. Smell good. See you in three years! Love, You." Oh good job, Emm. That was classic.

> (**MARCUS** and **COLBY** *applaud for him and laugh.*)

EMMETT. That felt a lot worse than I imagined it would.

MARCUS. I never thought you smelled bad. Did you, Colby?

COLBY. Ummm...

EMMETT. You thought I smelled bad?

COLBY. Not "bad." But you had a distinct scent for a while. It's not news to you! You wrote about it back then.

EMMETT. Fine. Marcus read Colby's. Now.

COLBY. I didn't write anything like that.

EMMETT. Well, let's see.

MARCUS. All right. Hold on to your butts. "Whattup Colby?? I HATE POKÉMON. I HATE POKÉMON. I HATE POKÉMON. I HATE POKÉMON. I HATE POKÉMON. –"

EMMETT. Is that seriously all he wrote?

COLBY. I told you. Sorry.

MARCUS. No, there's other stuff. But we said no editing. There are a couple more. "I HATE POKÉMON. I HATE POKÉMON." Okay we're done with that. He moves on.

"Okay that got boring.

Emmett is making us write letters to ourselves before we bury our broken Bionicles in his backyard. RIP Bionicles! This kid is ridiculous, but I love him. Whether he knows it or not, or likes it or not, one day he is going to be MINE. Haha! I am never letting him read this."

COLBY. Wait, what?

MARCUS. You already had a thing for Emmett?

COLBY. No. It wasn't like that back then.

MARCUS. I'll repeat: "This kid is ridiculous, but I love him. Whether he knows it or not, or likes it or not, one day he is going to be MINE. Haha! I am never letting him read this."

EMMETT. This was four years before anything started. Why didn't you say something sooner?

COLBY. I don't know. Maybe I was just waiting for you to discover Axe Body Spray.

EMMETT. Wow. Okay.

COLBY. I'm kidding. That was a joke. Come on.

MARCUS. Can I continue?

EMMETT. Yes.   **COLBY.** No.

MARCUS. Okay. "Questions for 2011: Is Barack Obama still president or did somebody kill him?"

EMMETT. Jeez, Colby!

COLBY. That was a legitimate concern!

MARCUS. "I hope he's alive. Everyone's so happy now. But I'm nervous. People in this country are assholes. But I'm glad people are happy about this. Are Mom and Dad still together? Do you want them to be? Let's hope our future selves fight less."

EMMETT. You thought they were getting divorced?

COLBY. I told you about that.

EMMETT. Not in a serious way.

COLBY. Maybe you didn't take it seriously.

MARCUS. But they are still together, right?

COLBY. Yeah, they're fine. I don't know. I guess I was just thinking about it that day and I needed to write something down. Can we finish this up? It's stupid.

MARCUS. "This letter is stupid. Nothing's even going to happen in three years. I should've told Emm we should dig this thing up after high school, but I don't plan on sticking around here after that and I want to be here to get my stuff back. I hope you're not still a virgin. Don't be a loser. Keep being awesome. WHY SO SERIOUS, SON? – COLBY." Oh you used to quote that all the time. "Why so serious, son?"

EMMETT. Yeah, misquoting *The Dark Knight* for seven years running.

COLBY. You know he says it that way once / when he's torturing that guy.

EMMETT. No, he says, "Why so seriousssuh"! With an extended "s" and no hard "n." You're not hearing it correctly.

COLBY. Well can you hear this correctly: Ssssuh! k'mydick.

MARCUS. You had that awesome Joker costume for Halloween that year, right? With the makeup?

COLBY. Yeah.

MARCUS. I was actually around for that one, right?

COLBY. Yeah, that was the month before we buried this thing. You were Batman. Emm was Two-Face.

MARCUS. Oh, yeah. That was great. We all had great costumes.

COLBY. Is that it for my letter?

MARCUS. That's all you wrote.

COLBY. Okay, Emm. Main event. Read us Marcus' letter.

EMMETT. Okay. "Dear Future Me, I'm writing a letter to you because Emmett asked me to. I'm thirteen. I'm sitting in our clubhouse. Right now, I only feel safe here. If I could live here instead of in my house, I would. Even if it kinda smells." – It smells in here?

COLBY. It doesn't smell. You smelled.

EMMETT. Goddammit. "Even if it kinda smells. And even if there's no bathroom. I'm not just saying that. Murray is an asshole. And Mom always takes his side on everything. I hope it's not still like that when you're reading this back. I really hope it's better. But right now, that's how it is. I wonder what Emmett and Colby are writing. Colby is writing some stupid shit because he has that dumb grin on his face like he's being so clever when he's not. Dude cannot tell a joke for his life and he thinks he's so hilarious. It almost becomes hilarious how unfunny he is, but not quite. No, I take it back. He's funny, I guess. Sometimes!"

COLBY. You didn't like my jokes?

MARCUS. You used to say these things and it was like you thought they were puns, but they weren't puns. They didn't make any sense. And you'd crack yourself up over them.

COLBY. Come on, I told good jokes!

EMMETT. No, Marcus is right. Let me keep going. "His mom makes the best brownies. Your record for brownies eaten in one sitting is six. I hope by now you're up to at least ten. Emmett looks really stressed right now. The letters were his idea! Why is he always stressing? He needs to relax. He is always nervous. Three years from now you'll be in a different school. What I really hope for is that when you read this in the future, it can still be like it is now. I hope we can all still be together. If that's how it turns out, I'd be happy. Because I don't know where else I can go. No one else has my back like these two. I know I can count on them. I know high school can change things, but I want to stay close. If we're still the Three Amigos, I think I could face anything.

"To wrap it up, join the soccer team! Go on a real date with Angela Bercy! Make that happen! Oh, and even though they're both really gay, Emmett and Colby should never date. That'd be awful. If you see it happening SHUT IT DOWN. GOBAMA!!! Forever, Marcus."

COLBY. Whoa, you didn't want us to go out?

MARCUS. I was probably nervous if you guys got together, then I'd be the third wheel. I didn't want to get shut out of our friendship. It was dumb of me to be worried. You guys were a good couple.

COLBY. Yeah, instead of you getting boxed out you became the center of everything. It's funny, isn't it? We all kinda got what we wanted.

EMMETT. What do you mean?

COLBY. You didn't want to smell bad anymore, I wanted you to be my boyfriend and Marcus wanted us to stay friends no matter what.

MARCUS. That's true... Could that be it?

EMMETT. You think the letters...

COLBY. What – are magic?

EMMETT. Well, maybe...

COLBY. No way. And my jokes were funny. They just went over your head.

MARCUS. Okay, Colbs.

EMMETT. Did you really feel that way? That no place else was safe for you?

MARCUS. Yeah. I really didn't like being at home. Murray was constantly on my ass about everything. Even me losing my school ID was this huge fight. And back then he had that hip surgery and he was always complaining he was in pain, and he couldn't get around. And that made him even more of an asshole. Are he and my mom still together?

EMMETT. What? Yeah. Why?

MARCUS. I just realized that I don't know anything real about them from the time I left. What I think they're doing now, it's all made up. What are they doing?

EMMETT. They live in your old house still. They...work.

MARCUS. That's it? Colby?

COLBY. What? I dunno.

MARCUS. Well, you haven't really missed an opportunity to throw something at me tonight. Are they alright?

COLBY. They're as good as to be expected given the circumstances.

MARCUS. Did people help them after I was gone?

EMMETT. People were very supportive.

COLBY. No, they weren't.

EMMETT. They were so!

COLBY. Emm, don't lie! People barely came out to search.

MARCUS. What?

EMMETT. That is so not true.

COLBY. It is true. People thought you ran away, so they just waited to see if you'd come back.

MARCUS. No one looked for me?

EMMETT. No, Colby is twisting everything. *We* saw you last in the woods that night, right? But we thought you just went home. And your mom thought you were sleeping over here, so she didn't expect you'd be around. So it was only when we came looking for you at the house the next day that we realized you weren't there and that you were really gone.

COLBY. But even at that point, nobody really looked for you.

EMMETT. We did so!

COLBY. I mean the cops. There was never a real search.

EMMETT. Colby, there was so a search. Why are you making it sound / like no one did anything?

MARCUS. Guys?

COLBY. By the time they took it seriously, they had waited too long.

EMMETT. They thought it was most likely that you ran away.

COLBY. Because that's what we told them!

MARCUS. You told them I ran away?

EMMETT. We never said we thought that's what happened. When you didn't show up we were afraid maybe you got hurt and were still out there. And our parents and your parents and *a lot of other people* went looking for you in the woods, but we couldn't find you. And the police asked us if we thought it was possible you ran away. But we never said we thought you did.

MARCUS. Is this one of the things you tell me every time I come back and I just forget or are you just getting around to sharing this part with me?

COLBY. No. We've never talked about it. Usually you don't want to know anything.

MARCUS. So, the police thought I ran away, and that's why they didn't look that hard for me at the beginning?

COLBY. Yes, and that was fucked up of them because there wasn't any other evidence that you'd run away. None of your things were missing. No money was missing from your house. Even if you had left home, how far were you going to get with no money, right?

EMMETT. Right...

COLBY. You didn't even own a sleeping bag. They knew you didn't run away. They were just looking for any excuse not to have to waste their time on you. This town has a lot more people like our old pal Aaron Brody in it. They just hide it better.

MARCUS. Wow... okay. Wow.

(**MARCUS** *retreats and considers this.*)

COLBY. It's true! They were all like, "Oh well. He ran off!" And that's it. Case closed. Black kid disappears, no big loss and everyone goes back to their own lives as fast as possible.

EMMETT. What are you talking about?

COLBY. Oh, Emm. I'm sorry, I thought you knew. Marcus is Black.

MARCUS. Colbs, man. Come on. I told you that in confidence.

EMMETT. Guys, stop fucking around! You're saying –

COLBY. I'm saying if it were you or me who disappeared instead of him, maybe they would've tried a little harder. But it wasn't. And they didn't.

EMMETT. That's not – people cared!

COLBY. *We* cared. But I think you need to go back and read through that scrapbook with a more discriminating eye. After Kasperak got caught, I did a deep dive into everything I could find online to see if what they were saying really fit. Most of the coverage leans heavily on the idea that Marcus ran away.

EMMETT. You're wrong.

(**EMMETT** *goes back to the scrapbook. Trying to find evidence in the articles.*)

COLBY. No, I'm not. Sorry, Marcus. The deck was already stacked against you from the moment you disappeared.

MARCUS. I know how that deck is stacked, thanks.

COLBY. Do you? Then why keep coming back to this? What'd you say earlier about not thinking about the world we go back to when you're not around? Well, spoiler alert – it's a shitty, racist place where no one looks for missing Black kids because you're not worth the time.

MARCUS. Dude, breathe.

COLBY. Why are you so calm about this? This is what pisses me off about you, Marcus. You should be so pissed off!

MARCUS. I'm –

COLBY. Get pissed off!

EMMETT. Colby, I don't think whatever therapy you're going to is actually helping.

COLBY. What's that supposed to mean?

MARCUS. It means you seem to have a lot of anger bottled up inside and tonight you're choosing to direct it all at me.

COLBY. I am angry! I'm disgusted. I'm most disgusted with myself.

MARCUS. Why?

COLBY. Because when I'm with you guys I forget about everything I know that's true, and instead I let myself believe all this stupid shit. I really thought that if we opened the time capsule you'd disappear and it'd be over.

And then I told myself, we'd go through everything, and there'd be a clue as to why you're here, but there isn't. And before all that, I told myself I would not get tricked into thinking you are really Marcus and I can't even do that for more than five minutes. You're standing there, totally perfect. You make me laugh...like, *really laugh*, and I – I can't beat you, whatever you are. You want us to come back every year and play pretend, fine. I just can't keep trying to make sense of you. It's too much.

MARCUS. I keep telling you. I'm your friend. I'm not a monster, Colby. You know that. Seriously, what else can I do?

COLBY. I just wish you...were all of you. I don't think what you show us is all of you.

MARCUS. You could say that about anybody.

COLBY. Yeah, I guess. I guess...

(**COLBY** *breaks down.*)

MARCUS. God, will you give yourself a break? Hey, Colbs? Come on.

COLBY. I'm sorry. I'm so sorry, Marcus.

MARCUS. Come on. Bring it in. Both arms this time.

(*They hug for a while.*)

COLBY. So that's everything, Emm? The time capsule's all empty now, huh?

(**EMMETT** *rummages through the bin.*)

EMMETT. There's a bunch of shredded paper I put at the bottom for the Bionicles. But yeah that's – wait! Something's taped to the bottom.

COLBY. What is it?

(**EMMETT** *pulls it out. It's another photograph.*)

EMMETT. It's the three of us! I put this in first before all the other stuff. Ha! Look at us!

MARCUS. Emm, your dad took this one at the party too!

COLBY. You wrote, "Best Friends Forever" on it. Really? Also for the love of god why do I look like I have a double chin?

MARCUS. Calm down. It's just the angle.

COLBY. I knew my angles back then! By the way, nice shirt, Marcus.

EMMETT. I think we look good! At least we're all happy!

COLBY. Yeah, where'd those kids go, huh?

MARCUS. Simpler times.

(**COLBY** *yawns.*)

Let's get ready for some shut-eye.

COLBY. No, I'm not closing my eyes on you.

MARCUS. Why? Afraid I'll expose my fangs and drain the blood from your body?

COLBY. No, I think you're gonna disappear. You never make it to morning.

MARCUS. Do I always sneak out in the middle of the night?

EMMETT. Kinda.

COLBY. You say goodbye to Emmett, but you don't say goodbye to me!

EMMETT. Because you're always asleep!

MARCUS. That hardly seems fair. Why would I do that?

EMMETT. Because Colby's not good at saying goodbye.

COLBY. Oh that's bullshit. I can handle saying goodbye. I want to make sure everything is copacetic between us before you go.

MARCUS. Ten points for "copacetic," State School!

COLBY. You know my vocabulary might have been shit when I was little, but it's improved in the *interceding* years.

MARCUS. I noticed. So you want things copacetic. Then what am I, Colby? Let me hear it loud and proud.

COLBY. You're my friend. Okay? I don't know what else you are or how you're here. But you're Marcus. You're my friend. I believe you.

MARCUS. Thank you. Now if the time comes for me to go and you're asleep, I promise to let you know this time and not just disappear. Okay?

COLBY. I'm not going to be asleep. I'm going to drink Coke, or coffee or keep my eyelids open with toothpicks if necessary.

EMMETT. Eww.

COLBY. Point is. This plays out with all of us together. I'm in it to the end.

> (*Lights dim. The* **GUYS** *get into the sleeping bags.* **COLBY** *yawns and lies down and falls asleep on his back. Lights go back up.* **EMMETT** *watches* **COLBY** *sleep as* **MARCUS** *pages through the scrapbook.*)

Scene Three

EMMETT. I'm surprised he's not snoring. He usually snores when he's on his back like that.

MARCUS. Life's full of miracles. He looks really peaceful.

EMMETT. Looks can be deceiving. What are you reading in there?

MARCUS. Nothing really. Just looking through. It's weird.

EMMETT. Yeah, I bet.

MARCUS. A lot of it's really old. Except for the really new stuff.

EMMETT. Well, the case has been cold for a long time. Until Kasperak and the bodies.

MARCUS. I don't really feel connected to any of this. It's just a record of my absence.

EMMETT. I guess that's true. You thinking about what Colby said?

MARCUS. I'm thinking about my mom in relation to what Colby said.

EMMETT. Well, talk to me. What's going on?

MARCUS. When Colby was going off I had this weird flash of watching my mom cleaning out pots in our kitchen sink after dinner. It was my job to dry. As I was waiting, I liked watching how she scrubbed them. You know when the soap hits the grease and it just makes that vooo...

(He gestures with his hands to show an expanding circle.)

It just rushes out from the center so quickly?

EMMETT. Yeah.

MARCUS. Well that's the image that came to mind when Colby brought it up. A drop of soap hitting greasy water and then my mom's face. It changes how I remember things. And I keep thinking about her looking at a sink of dirty dishes.

EMMETT. In your head, how does she look?

MARCUS. Tired, kinda overwhelmed, but determined. I bet that's her face all the time now. It's been her only face for six years. She doesn't know what happened to me. She doesn't know why it happened. I can see her reading these articles when they came out and her not knowing if the people who were supposed to find me were really trying. I can't do anything for her. And now...

EMMETT. What? Say it.

MARCUS. I really feel lost. I'm not with my dad. I can't be with my mom. I'm no place.

EMMETT. You're right here.

MARCUS. Do you think Colby's right? Do you think that's why they never found me?

EMMETT. I really don't know. I mean, yes. Maybe. I'm second guessing everything that happened now. Everything we did. I feel like I know less now than I ever did about any of this.

MARCUS. And you came into tonight hoping for answers.

EMMETT. Well, *Colby* did, at least. What were you hoping for?

MARCUS. Just homemade brownies from his mom.

EMMETT. Well, at least you're not strangers to disappointment. I don't want it to be true. That doesn't make it untrue. It could've been because you're Black, they didn't look hard enough. It could be other things too.

MARCUS. Why don't I know what happened to me? I keep looking inside myself for the answers. They're not there. What does that mean?

EMMETT. It just means…you don't know.

(**MARCUS** *closes the scrapbook and pushes it away from him. He notices* **EMMETT** *watching* **COLBY**.)

MARCUS. Do you think he's awake and just listening to us?

EMMETT. Huh?

MARCUS. You keep gazing at him.

EMMETT. Gazing? No. It's just… it's stupid.

MARCUS. No, come on. Share and share alike.

EMMETT. I can't believe he wrote that about me in his letter.

MARCUS. Why not?

EMMETT. Well, for starters, I wasn't some big prize.

MARCUS. Colby's not out of your league, dude. He never was.

EMMETT. Shall I show you the picture of us at thirteen again?

MARCUS. I've seen that picture. Colby *does* have a double chin.

EMMETT. I'm worried about him.

MARCUS. He has a lot to work through. He needs time. And a better therapist.

EMMETT. Did you check his brain when he said his parents were moving? That was a lie, right?

MARCUS. I did not look in his brain. I don't actively root around in there for either of you, despite what you believe.

EMMETT. Well, that's what it looks like you're doing. Looking into us.

MARCUS. Well, *looks* can be deceiving.

EMMETT. Touché.

MARCUS. You think he was lying?

EMMETT. I know he wants to get away from here. And I know he wants closure. So maybe he just said that to force the issue.

MARCUS. Speaking of closure, are you going to tell him that you're dating somebody?

EMMETT. Hey! Not cool! You just said –

MARCUS. I didn't have to dig around in your brain to know *that*. When I asked him earlier if he was dating anyone, you got all weird. He probably assumes it's because he hurt you, but I think it's because you're the one who moved on. Am I right?

EMMETT. It's new. That's why I didn't invite Colby to *The Seagull*. I just…couldn't have them in the same place. Not yet.

MARCUS. Tell me about him.

EMMETT. He's nice! He's a year above me, so he's gonna be a senior next year. He did the lighting design for the show. We like the same stuff. It's nice.

MARCUS. What's his name?

EMMETT. Allistar.

MARCUS. Allistar? Well, that's a name.

EMMETT. It is! Shut up. I like his name.

MARCUS. Is he rich? Allistar sounds like a rich person name.

EMMETT. I don't think he's that rich. I don't know. I haven't asked to see his parents' tax returns yet. We're not at that level.

MARCUS. But you're happy?

EMMETT. It's okay.

MARCUS. Good. You should tell Colbs about him.

EMMETT. Hmph. Why?

MARCUS. Because you're letting him feel guilty about hurting you, and if he knew you were moving on, he'd feel better.

EMMETT. I told him I was over it.

MARCUS. It's not the same thing. You see how much guilt he carries around about everything. Be honest about it. You love him, so even if it's fun to torture him a bit when he's a jerk, lighten the load when you can.

EMMETT. I liked it more when we were little and you just automatically took my side on everything.

MARCUS. I'm still on your side.

> (**COLBY** *whimpers and turns on his side in a more fetal position. His head rolls off his pillow.* **EMMETT** *watches him and smiles.*)

EMMETT. Each year it's been harder than the one before to get him to go along with this. I think he wants so badly to either believe in you or hate you, but he can't reconcile what it is that's happening. He got his hopes up about Kasperak.

MARCUS. But not you. You don't think he's a part of it?

EMMETT. If I believed in Kasperak then I'd have to believe you died. And I don't believe you died.

MARCUS. How do you explain to yourself what happened to me? I'm sure you came up with some story. What was the story?

EMMETT. I like to think that on that night you were running home through the woods and you took a wrong turn and went deeper in than we'd ever gone before. And then you came across some hidden portal, some dimensional tear and you fell through and wound up in this other world I called, "Perchance." I'd write stories about it. It had all these fantasy elements. There was a wizard who used a magic spell to summon you there to be their champion. You started as a knight's apprentice and then became a knight. I had this whole series mapped out. You were a hero there. You were happy. And you forgot all about your old life here. We became just a dream for you. But every year on the anniversary of when you disappeared, you'd fall into a deep trance-like sleep and the magic that took you away would bring you back to us and you'd be your true self. Our friend, as you should've been. Just for one night and then you'd get whisked away back to chasing glory in that other land.

MARCUS. I really like that.

EMMETT. It's not real though.

MARCUS. Why not?

EMMETT. It's just something I made up.

MARCUS. There's gotta be some magic in this world, Emmett. Look at us.

EMMETT. Yeah, look at us.

MARCUS. So there's something else we need to talk about.

EMMETT. What?

MARCUS. Your allowance.

EMMETT. Yeah, I don't get an allowance anymore. I work now.

MARCUS. I know, but you used to and you hid it out here in the clubhouse so that Jamie wouldn't steal it from you.

EMMETT. It didn't really stop her though –

MARCUS. You kept it in the Game of Life box. You had seventy-eight dollars tucked away in there in eighth grade.

EMMETT. Okay. How do you know that?

MARCUS. Because I took it. You know I did. You can stop being polite about it.

EMMETT. I didn't…

MARCUS. Emm, you know.

EMMETT. After you disappeared, I checked for it and it was gone. But a bunch of people knew I kept it out here. They could've taken it a bunch of times.

MARCUS. Every time I come back here we play Life. Every year, I see a real wad of money rolled up in the box.

EMMETT. I don't keep my money out here anymore –

MARCUS. And then I win and I put the board away and I always take the money with me. It's right here. I can show you.

(*He goes to take out the money.*)

EMMETT. No.

MARCUS. Why not?

EMMETT. I don't know. Just don't.

(**EMMETT** *moves away from* **MARCUS.**)

MARCUS. There's so many things we can't be certain about, but there's this thing, between you and me, I need to be settled. We've come all this way. Why can't we?

EMMETT. Because it doesn't mean anything.

MARCUS. It does. It means something to us.

(**MARCUS** *takes the money out of his pocket.*)

Here. See? It's true. I took it. Do you hate me now?

EMMETT. I don't hate you. Why did you take it?

MARCUS. Just to have it. It sounds stupid saying it. It wasn't about needing money. It had nothing to do with that. I wanted it because it was yours and it was *right there* and knowing I could take it and have it without you knowing – I couldn't stop myself. Maybe that's why Colby took our cards back then too. I don't know. I just needed to know what it felt like to take it. I immediately felt so guilty. I never could've spent it. I wanted to put it back, but I couldn't find a chance. So I was holding it until I could do it without you seeing and then I still had it on me that night.

EMMETT. So you weren't going to run away with it?

MARCUS. No! It has nothing to do with that. I'm really sorry. Do you forgive me?

EMMETT. Of course I forgive you. Do you forgive me?

MARCUS. For what?

EMMETT. Because it was me. Colby and your family didn't think there was money missing, so they didn't think you ran away, but when I saw the money was gone, I wasn't sure. And the cops must've been able to tell. They knew I believed it was possible you ran away and it affected the whole search.

MARCUS. No. You can't keep thinking that. You were just a kid, Emm. We were all just little kids. We didn't know anything. I want you to take it back.

(**MARCUS** *extends the money to him.*)

EMMETT. What?

MARCUS. Take it back. I don't want it anymore. How many problems has it caused for us?

EMMETT. I can't just take it from you, Marcus. Nothing from you ever stays here once you go. It won't stay. It won't mean anything.

MARCUS. Why not? Why can't we say how it works? Just turn around and don't look and I'll put it back in the box and it'll be like it didn't happen.

EMMETT. But it did happen.

MARCUS. So I hold on to it forever? We might not get another chance at this.

> (**EMMETT** *thinks. He has an idea. He gets the Game of Life box and brings it to* **MARCUS.** *He opens the lid.*)

EMMETT. It did happen. We can't pretend it didn't. So we'll face it.

> (**MARCUS** *holds out the money over the box. He has difficulty relaxing his grip on the money. Eventually he does drop it in.* **EMMETT** *closes the lid.*)

MARCUS. There! I did it!

EMMETT. Feel better?

MARCUS. Yeah, I feel a lot lighter. That was weighing me down.

> (**MARCUS** *and* **EMMETT** *smile at each other until they sense a change of energy in the air.* **EMMETT** *yawns.*)

EMMETT. Crash with us this time. You brought the bag.

MARCUS. I think maybe I should pack up and go now. I think it's time.

EMMETT. Now? I hoped we could –

MARCUS. I know. The wizard is calling me back, I think. Perchance needs its hero knight to slay a marauding dragon or beat back a robot army or something better only you could come up with.

(**EMMETT***'s face falls.*)

What's wrong?

(**EMMETT** *brightens again, smiling.*)

EMMETT. Nothing!

MARCUS. Why do you do that?

EMMETT. What?

MARCUS. Put on that fake smile when you're sad.

EMMETT. I've found, over time, it's a solid coping mechanism.

MARCUS. Just be sad. You can be real about it.

EMMETT. No. I don't want to be sad around you. I want you to have the best night possible. I want to be able to give that to you.

MARCUS. You do. You always make me feel great, Emm.

EMMETT. Yeah, but it's not enough.

MARCUS. Not enough for who?

EMMETT. For me. You – No, I don't want to do this.

(*He turns away from* **MARCUS.**)

MARCUS. Emm, why didn't you dig up the time capsule when you were supposed to? Why say no every year and then do it now but not tell anybody?

EMMETT. Because I knew if Colby and I had dug it up, that would be over. And I didn't want it to be over. I was trying to give us a chance. I was... We all just had to keep going. If the three of us couldn't be here to dig it up together, it was just gonna stay down there forever. But then Colby broke up with me, and I couldn't see a way to keep the three of us going anymore. I felt so...

MARCUS. Betrayed?

EMMETT. Yes, like he betrayed us. And I didn't know what to do. And then this spring, I saw my dad working in the ground where we buried it and I was like, "Fuck it. I'll just get it and go through it all myself." But when it came to me actually opening it, I couldn't do it. It felt wrong. So I stored it in here and I went back to school and I figured that's where it would stay.

But then they found the bodies out behind Forrester, which made Colby and I start talking again and I knew he'd come back this time if only to ask you about Kasperak. So I saw a way we could keep it going a little longer. I like when you come back. I look forward to it.

MARCUS. And now it's complete.

EMMETT. No.

MARCUS. Why not?

EMMETT. Because we didn't win! *We didn't win.* I should be able to hold on to you and pull you back. You should be here. You should stay. We've earned that!

*(He cries. **MARCUS** holds him.)*

It wasn't supposed to be like this.

MARCUS. Well…that's how things work out sometimes.

EMMETT. You know when being comforted, it helps to not have your own words from earlier thrown back at you?

MARCUS. Yeah, I can see how that might sting.

EMMETT. It's not fair. And I'm not okay with it.

MARCUS. No one here's asking you to be.

*(They sit together for a moment silently, content in their own company. **MARCUS** starts humming a tune.* The melody is clear to him. Less so to **EMMETT**.)*

---

* A license to produce *A Burial Place* does not include a performance license for any third-party or copyrighted music.

EMMETT. Are you attempting the *Smash Bros.* theme song?

MARCUS. Yeah!

(**EMMETT** *shakes his head.*)

What?

EMMETT. You're off pitch and off-tempo.

MARCUS. Bullshit. That's the tune. Where's my kazoo? I'll play it on that.

EMMETT. Please, no. That would be too much to bear right now.

MARCUS. Okay, then. Back to silence.

(*They sit for a moment.* **MARCUS** *starts rolling up his sleeping bag.*)

EMMETT. They're not gonna find your body out in the woods, are they?

(**MARCUS** *pauses. Thinks about this.*)

MARCUS. I don't think so. But hey – stranger things have happened, right?

(*They separate and stand up.*)

EMMETT. So, that's it. You're going.

MARCUS. It's time.

EMMETT. What should we do with your stuff from the time capsule?

MARCUS. Can you bring it to my mom? She might like to have it back.

EMMETT. What about the letter?

MARCUS. No, not the letter. I don't want her to read that. Burn it. Burn it and bury the ashes under the clubhouse. Put it to rest.

EMMETT. You sure?

MARCUS. Yeah, that feels right.

EMMETT. Okay. But I'm keeping the can!

MARCUS. You better.

> (**MARCUS** *hugs* **EMMETT**. *It goes on for a moment.*)

EMMETT. Wait. Since your pockets are a little lighter. Take this with you.

> (**EMMETT** *hands* **MARCUS** *the picture of the three of them from the time capsule.*)

MARCUS. You sure?

EMMETT. Something to remember us by.

MARCUS. That'd be nice. Thanks... You know what? I really think there's something still out there for me. See you around, Emm.

EMMETT. Bye, Marcus. Stay safe out there, okay?

MARCUS. Okay. Hey, do me a favor? Keep writing those stories.

> (**MARCUS** *looks at* **COLBY** *sleeping. He picks up* **COLBY**'s *pillow and hits him with it as he heads for the door.*)

COLBY. Hey!

MARCUS. Stop snoring.

> (**COLBY** *rubs his eyes.* **EMMETT** *laughs.* **MARCUS** *smiles and exits.*)

COLBY. I wasn't even snoring! Was I?

EMMETT. No, you weren't.

COLBY. So stop laughing. Why'd you – where is he?

EMMETT. He's gone, babe.

COLBY. Gone? You let him go?

(**COLBY** *runs out the door.*)

EMMETT. What was I supposed to do? Tackle him?

COLBY. *(Offstage.)* MARCUS! MARCUS, GET BACK HERE! YOU HEAR ME?

EMMETT. Colby, get the fuck back inside! My parents are gonna hear you! The whole neighborhood is gonna hear.

COLBY. *(Offstage.)* Fuck!

EMMETT. C'mon, Colby!

(**COLBY** *re-enters.*)

COLBY. Fuck! GODDAMIT! What did he say?

EMMETT. He said to keep writing stories about him.

COLBY. That's it? How could you let him go when he didn't tell us anything?

EMMETT. He told us what he knew.

(**EMMETT** *goes and picks up Marcus' letter and the paper stuffing from the time capsule. He continues to walk around the room getting the garbage can and the lighter.*)

COLBY. So that's it? We're done. It's all over.

EMMETT. Not quite.

(*He drops the shavings from the time capsule and Marcus' letter in the bucket and lights it. The bucket glows.*)

COLBY. What are you doing?

EMMETT. Proper burial. Ashes to ashes. Dust to dust.

> *(He goes and picks up the other two letters.
> Hands **COLBY** his. Drops his own in the
> bucket.)*

COLBY. You didn't want to keep it?

EMMETT. They belong together.

> *(**COLBY** considers this. Drops his own letter
> in the mix.)*

COLBY. Poof. Okay. Anything else?

EMMETT. Yeah, if it's there.

> *(**EMMETT** goes and gets the Game of Life box.)*

COLBY. You're gonna torch the game?

EMMETT. No!

COLBY. Oh. Too bad.

> *(**EMMETT** takes out the wad of cash that's in
> the box.)*

EMMETT. It's still here!

COLBY. You still hide your money in that game box?

EMMETT. Not anymore.

> *(**EMMETT** drops the money into the fire in the
> can.)*

COLBY. I'm pretty sure burning the game was the smarter
move there, Emm.

EMMETT. C'mon. What else? Is that everything?

COLBY. The scrapbook?

> *(**EMMETT** stops. He picks it up off the ground.)*

EMMETT. Oh, god. The scrapbook? I don't know.

COLBY. It's not evidence.

EMMETT. I know.

COLBY. Who are we really keeping it for?

> (**EMMETT** *drops it in the bucket. They watch it burn.*)

We can always pull the info up online, if we need it again.

EMMETT. I'm dating someone.

COLBY. Um. Okay. Is he into threesomes?

EMMETT. No, Colby.

COLBY. Bummer. Why are you telling me?

EMMETT. I don't know. To tell you. Is it weird?

COLBY. Yes. If you're happy, I'm happy. But I'm kinda processing a lot right now, so I reserve the right to find whoever-he-is unworthy of you at a later date and time. Okay?

EMMETT. I'll take it. Are your folks really moving to Virginia Beach?

COLBY. Yeah, Emm. They are.

EMMETT. Oh, I thought maybe you were just…

COLBY. No. Sorry. What do we do when the fire burns down?

EMMETT. We're gonna bury the ashes outside.

COLBY. What are we gonna do in the meantime?

> (*They look at each other.*)

EMMETT. S'mores!   **COLBY.** S'mores!

> (*They run to get the marshmallows.*)

EMMETT. Untwist those hangers!

> (**COLBY** *works to unbend two wire hangers hanging on the nail in the wall.*)

COLBY. Do you think the fire will last long enough?

EMMETT. Hurry and we'll see!

> (**EMMETT** *sticks two marshmallows on the ends of the wires and they sit down and roast them.*)

COLBY. Victory!

EMMETT. At last!

> (*They holler and laugh. It's a big release for them. They hug each other fiercely, as if afraid it might be for the last time. They sit for a moment in silence.*)

COLBY. They're gonna find his body, Emm. He's out there.

EMMETT. He's somewhere. But not here anymore.

> (*They share another moment of silence.*)

COLBY. You're going to invite me to see your play in the fall, right?

EMMETT. Sure.

COLBY. Do I get to know what it's about?

EMMETT. It's about...an adventure.

> (*They lean on each other and watch the fire burn down.*)

End of Play